## "They have Hope, Chance's sh...

"The kidnappers rode off into the wilderness with Hope! They told me I'll never see her again unless I convince you to change your mind about testifying! Oh, God...what are we going to do?"

Panic rose in Pru at the very thought of her daughter's fate in the kidnapper's hands. Hope's screams at being ripped away from the comfort of her mother's arms echoed in Pru's head. They'd haunted every moment of her wild ride to find help, and probably would stay with her until her child was safe in her arms once more.

"I'm going to find her," Chance said, his expression grim. Then he kissed her forehead comfortingly. "I'm here for you, Pru."

"I knew I could count on you, Chance," she murmured, looking deeply into his eyes. "I knew I could trust you." He drew her in. How could she have doubted him, even for a moment? "I always knew in my heart that you were a good man."

Only a really good man would volunteer to go find a child he didn't even know was his....

Dear Reader,

I've always thought that if I were to move from Chicago, it would be to northern New Mexico. I love the look and the feel of the place—the brilliant sunny skies with a clear light that inspires me, the rugged landscapes that remind me of a past that I still romanticize as I did when I was a kid.

And so it was an exceptional pleasure for me to bring a bit of that romanticized past to my latest Harlequin Intrigue book. The SONS OF SILVER SPRINGS—half brothers Bart, Chance and Reed—return to save the Curly-Q Ranch despite bitter memories of each other and their relationship with their father, who is dying. In doing so, they find not only danger and the loves of their lives, but a new respect for family and tradition.

If you enjoy their ride, please let me know—
P.O. Box 578297, Chicago, IL 60657-8297.
Send an SASE for information on upcoming books.

Regards,

*Patricia Rosemoor*

# The Lone Wolf's Child
## Patricia Rosemoor

HARLEQUIN®

TORONTO • NEW YORK • LONDON
AMSTERDAM • PARIS • SYDNEY • HAMBURG
STOCKHOLM • ATHENS • TOKYO • MILAN • MADRID
PRAGUE • WARSAW • BUDAPEST • AUCKLAND

ISBN 0-373-22563-6

THE LONE WOLF'S CHILD

Copyright © 2000 by Patricia Pinianski

This edition published by arrangement with Harlequin Books S.A.

® and TM are trademarks of the publisher. Trademarks indicated with ® are registered in the United States Patent and Trademark Office, the Canadian Trade Marks Office and in other countries.

Visit us at www.eHarlequin.com

**Printed in U.S.A.**

## ABOUT THE AUTHOR

Patricia Rosemoor is the recipient of the 1997 Career Achievement Award in Romantic Suspense from *Romantic Times Magazine*.

To research her novels, Patricia is willing to swim with dolphins, round up mustangs or howl with wolves—"whatever it takes to write a credible tale." She even went to jail for a day—as a guest of Cook County—to research a proposal.

Ms. Rosemoor holds a Master of Television degree and a B.A. degree in American literature from the University of Illinois. She lives in Chicago with her husband, Edward, and their three cats.

## Books by Patricia Rosemoor

### HARLEQUIN INTRIGUE

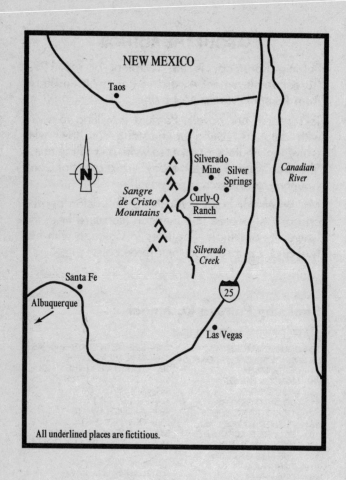

NEW MEXICO

Taos

**N**

Sangre
de Cristo
Mountains

Silverado
Mine
Silver
Springs

Curly-Q
Ranch

Canadian
River

Silverado
Creek

Santa Fe

Albuquerque

25

Las Vegas

All underlined places are fictitious.

# CAST OF CHARACTERS

*Chance Quarrels* — The youngest of the Quarrels brothers has two reasons for returning to Silver Springs and the Curly-Q Ranch — a place to hide out and the woman he loves.

*Prudence Prescott* — The mother of Chance's secret child tries to keep her emotional distance...until their daughter is kidnapped.

*Emmett Quarrels* — Chance's father fears his own secrets have put his son's life in danger.

*The Cowboy Poet* — The villain uses poetry to warn Chance from his purpose.

*Kleef Hatsfield* — The new day worker on the Curly-Q is around whenever bad things happen.

*Hugh Ruskin* — The bartender is sly about getting information.

*Will "Billy Boy" Spencer* — The former bronc rider has his own secrets to hide...like why he's working on the Curly-Q.

More thanks to Bryan and Kathy Turner
of Rancho Cañón Ancho for giving me
"dangerous ideas"...

# *Prologue*

As Chance Quarrels strolled into The Arena—a big, noisy bar at the outskirts of Trinity, New Mexico, famous for gut-burning chili and boot-tapping music—he stretched his mouth into a wide grin. He had cause to celebrate, didn't he? Wouldn't do to let on any differently.

"Well, if it ain't the big winner!" another rough-stock competitor loudly declared upon setting eyes on him. "You gonna share the wealth, boy?"

"Why not…?"

He'd won all three of his events. Normally he only rode bronc, both saddle and bareback, but today—even knowing he was probably out of his mind—he'd taken on a bull, as well. In addition to the nice fat purse, he'd limped away from that event with a pulled shoulder.

Not that the rest of him didn't ache, too, he thought, saying, "The next round's on me!"

Chance glanced over at a sea of rodeo acquaintances. He knew everyone, and everyone knew him. Mr. Popularity. A few cowboys whooped and hollered at the drink announcement, and a big-haired blonde sashayed right up to him so close he could count every lengthened, thickened lash around her beautiful doe-brown eyes.

"Congratulations, Chance," the rodeo groupie who called herself Silky murmured huskily, before throwing her arms around his neck and planting a big one on him.

It was easiest to let her kiss him. And from the way she pressed her body to his, Chance had no doubts she was willing and eager to extend her best wishes in a far more personal way than was possible in a public place. Wolf whistles from every corner of the room told him he wasn't the only one aware of her intentions.

Strangely unaffected, Chance put Silky from him. She was only after him because he was the big winner of the day, and if she got him into bed, that would make her a big winner in buckle bunny circles.

"Why, thank you, Silky, darlin'," he said with a slow smile and slower wink. "Now what can I get you? From the bar, that is?"

His way of putting her off without embarrassing her.

"A bottle of champagne...in my room?"

The last place he wanted to be. But obviously she wasn't easily discouraged.

"A bottle of your best champagne for the lady," Chance told the bartender. To Silky he said, "At the moment I'm in the mood for some line dancing." He indicated the crowded dance floor.

"You go ahead, then." The blonde settled back against a stool, then stretched her arms upward so that her large breasts practically spilled from her low-cut top. Pouting her full lips, she blew him a kiss from a hand heavy with gold and diamond ring.

"You come find me when you're in the mood for some *horizontal* dancing."

"I'll do that," Chance said smoothly.

He moved away from the woman who had a penchant only for winners. A while back he'd heard Silky had found herself permanent company...until the company had been taken out of the competitive field by a bull with sharp horns. He didn't need a woman like that.

Once on the dance floor, he joined the line of men and women, mostly other rodeo competitors, who were executing a complicated progression of steps to a wailing country tune. Within seconds Chance picked up the beat and kicked his heels with the best of them, all his aches and pains merely assuring him he was still alive.

His intention was to lose himself in the music and movement so he wouldn't have to think about a certain red-haired woman, the only one he did want to engage in a horizontal tango. But the more he tried putting her out of his mind, the more she plagued him.

Chance kicked harder, forced already-sore limbs into higher swings and harder stomps, raised a sweat so thick he felt as if he was in a boiler room, before the music stopped. Then he avoided another overly friendly female and sought out a smaller bar at the back of the place where he ordered a beer.

It was quieter back here, his memories louder. He resumed thinking about her; he could almost smell her scent, like dewy flower petals on—

A broadcast voice from the television above the bar cut into his thoughts.

"...interrupt our regular programming with a

news flash. Earlier today a security guard was shot when two masked men robbed the Stockman's Bank of Trinity…''

Pulse jagging, Chance flipped his attention to the television. The reporter was standing outside the bank in question. Behind her, a yellow Crime Scene tape kept the spectators back from the building.

And then the visual switched…

A security camera had caught the robbers, who wore cowboy hats and had wrapped bandannas around their lower faces.

For a moment the rushing in his ears blotted out all other sound. Then Chance snapped to, shook his head and forced himself to concentrate on what the reporter was saying as the camera came back to her.

''…Julio Alvarez was rushed to Trinity Hospital where, just a few minutes ago, he succumbed to his wounds. He leaves behind a wife and five small children….''

''Here you go, pal.'' The bartender set his draft on the bar before Chance. ''You don't look so good.''

Chance focused on the rough features under the silver buzz cut—they were pulled with concern.

Then he lied. ''Thanks, but I'm fine.'' And watched the rest of the bulletin with growing horror.

He wasn't fine at all. How could he be?

A guard shot and killed…he couldn't possibly have foreseen that.

What the hell was he going to do now?

# Chapter One

The roar of an engine made Prudence Prescott glance out the kitchen window to see a truck pull up and her brother-in-law alight. Dark-haired, solidly built Mitch Garner slipped an arm around Justine's waist and gave his wife an affectionate squeeze and a quick kiss.

And Pru quickly glanced away from the happy couple, her gaze settling on the three little girls playing in the side yard. Redheads all, they looked like stepping stones—Blythe was five, Fancy was three and Hope was nineteen months, two weeks and three days. The girls ran to greet Mitch, all screaming like little banshees.

Full lips softly curving in a smile, Pru turned her concentration to the task at hand—unloading the dishwasher.

She lived with her sister and brother-in-law, a convenient arrangement for them all. Sometimes she did more than her share in taking care of the place. As much as she hated being domesticated, she saw it as righteous payback.

She'd just emptied the bottom basket and was

working on the top when her sister slammed through the back door.

Justine Garner's face was flushed nearly as red as her hair—she was clearly agitated. "Pru, you'll never guess who just drove through town."

"You're right, I won't," Pru said, her gaze automatically going to the window to make sure that Mitch was entertaining the girls. "So tell me."

"Chance Quarrels." And when Justine asked, "What are you going to do about it?" a jar managed to slip through Pru's fingers.

Pru stared stupidly as the glass hit the sand-colored ceramic floor and shattered into hundreds of shards.

"Only one thing *to* do," she muttered, hardly breathing. "Clean up this mess."

Justine was already fetching the dustpan and whisk broom. "That's not what I meant and you know it."

Taking the implements from her sister's hand, Pru stared into hazel eyes so like her own. "What did you expect me to say?"

"That you'll talk to him—"

"When hell freezes over!"

"Don't let Papa hear you talk like that."

As if he hadn't heard worse from her in her wilder days. Pru stooped to sweep up the glass shards, muttering, "Well, Papa's not here at the moment, is he?"

The Reverend and Mrs. Brewster Prescott didn't even live in Silver Springs anymore. A virtual ghost town couldn't support a minister, and yet her father had hung on for more financially draining years than had been wise. Finally he'd made the move to a more viable town nearly an hour's drive south. Even so, he held services in Silver Springs every other Sunday afternoon because he couldn't let down the handful of older people who still wanted a place to worship and couldn't afford the time or energy to drive to another town. Pru and Justine and their mother Naomi shared the responsibility of keeping the small church usable.

As Pru rose and crossed to the mudroom where she dumped the glass into the garbage can, Justine shadowed her. "Honey, you've got to be reasonable."

"Do I?"

"It's only right."

"Right?" Incredulous, Pru glared at her sister. "Like Chance's leaving Silver Springs every time he gets an itchy foot? *That* kind of right?"

"But he didn't know—"

"What? That I loved him as much as he said he loved me?" Stalking back into the kitchen—a modernized if plain room with long counters, pine cabinets and table, Pru snorted and muttered, "That sure was a big fat lie."

"You don't know that."

"His not so much as calling me for nearly two and a half years is a pretty good indication."

Trying to deny the feelings her sister pricked, Pru relieved the dishwasher of the last few items and began shoving things in the cabinets.

"That's just Chance," Justine went on. "He's been drifting back and forth between the Curly-Q and who-knows-where since he finished school. He's been gone and back more times than I can count. You knew that when you got involved with him again. Just like you knew this day would come, that he would be back. He *always* comes back. And you know it won't be long before he comes for you, like always."

"Well, this time he can't have me!"

Pru slammed a stack of plates into a cabinet so hard they clattered against one another.

"What about his daughter?"

"He *definitely* can't have her!" Pru couldn't help the note of panic rising in her voice. "Chance doesn't know about Hope, and he's not going to!"

"But, Pru—"

"No! It was bad enough the way he left me." She'd finally given him her trust only to have him do his usual disappearing act. "I won't have him worming his way into my little girl's heart just so he can break hers, too!" Finally forgetting about the damn dishes, she faced her sister square and gave her the evil eye, just as she used to do when they were kids. "Justine Garner, the day I told you I was pregnant, you promised me you wouldn't tell Chance. Swear to me now that you won't break that promise."

Her sister appeared pained—torn—but in the end, she caved. "You know I won't."

"And Mitch?"

"I'll make sure."

No one else in town knew anything for certain. Pru hadn't shown until she was six months along, and by that time she'd gone to live with her parents, then had stayed for several months after giving birth. Hope was small for her age. Pru figured that anyone speculating would think she got pregnant by some stranger while she'd been gone.

"But our keeping your secret is no guarantee,"

Justine warned her. "Chance could take one look at that little girl and know she's his."

Pru joined her sister where she now stood, staring out the window. Sighing, she sought out her daughter. With her red hair and sunny freckled face, Hope was a Prescott through and through. Anyone seeing her with Blythe and Fancy would think the three little girls were sisters.

"She doesn't look a bit like Chance or any other Quarrels," Pru said more calmly than she was feeling.

"Hope has Chance's eyes, Pru. If he looks deep, he'll know."

"Then I just won't let him get close enough."

"To Hope? Or to you?"

"To either of us!"

"Brave words. And familiar."

But this time Pru was determined. This time she had reason to keep her distance—protecting her daughter from harm and disappointment being the most important reason she could think of. Hope didn't need a Chance Quarrels shaking up her safe little world.

Even so, as she watched Mitch swing Hope up into his arms as if she were one of his own girls, Pru ached for a man with teasing blue eyes, an easy smile, thick golden-brown hair that streaked light in the sun so that a woman was hard-pressed not to run her fingers through it.

Chance Quarrels...the love of her life...the only man who'd ever meant anything to her.

A man whose heart she could never possess.

That knowledge left an ache in her, big and hungry and acute.

That knowledge also made her angry, not because Chance couldn't give her what she'd wanted, but because he'd made her believe he had.

She'd been crazy over him probably longer than she could remember. Before he'd even noticed her. But she'd been a wild child, the despair of her preacher papa. Eventually she'd made sure Chance noticed.

They'd been good together. He'd understood her contrary nature and had been entertained by it. In return he'd made her heart sing. He'd made her feel as if he was the only man who could fill that space inside her—the part that was lonely and lost when he left.

And every time he'd come back from wherever he'd drifted, she'd taken up with him like he'd never been gone.

*But not this time.*

He'd never been gone this long before, Pru thought. More than two years. She'd begun to think he'd finally settled someplace else, away from his problematic family.

Away from *her.*

Now here he was, back again, big as life, just like his brother, Bart. Pru had heard about old Emmett being sick, but she couldn't feature that as a reason for Chance to jump. He had never been close to his father. And he had never wanted to settle in one place for long.

So, despite her determination to keep her distance from the man, Pru couldn't help wondering about the *real* reason Chance Quarrels had returned this time.

THE CURLY-Q HAD ALWAYS BEEN a haven, had always been a place to cool his heels. And his heels needed cooling real bad, Chance thought, as he stepped out of his truck to survey the spread below him.

Nestled in the canyon that cradled Silverado Creek, Curly-Q land went for miles in either direction. Chance stepped right to the rim fringed with cedar and juniper and, with his eyes, followed the zigzag road down the nearly thousand feet to buildings that looked like a kid's toys.

House. Barn. Bunkhouse. Storage shed.

All his—rather one-third his someday, if he signed on to a rancher's life for real.

Pa's lawyer Howard Siles had caught up with Chance at the rodeo grounds the week before to inform him that Emmett Quarrels had a heart condition and was living on borrowed time.

His pa dying…

He wouldn't think about that. He'd always kept a powder keg of emotions locked up tight inside him where Pa was concerned, and he didn't see any reason to loose them now.

Wanting his sons around him in his waning days, Pa had decided to have family corporation papers drawn up. Blindsided by his father's illness, Chance hadn't even looked the papers over properly before signing, but Siles had explained that the old man would turn over the Curly-Q and the property he owned in Silver Springs to him and his two half brothers for agreeing to work the spread.

The excuse to return to the Curly-Q was as good as any, he guessed. His father and brothers didn't have to know the *true* reason. So he'd signed the damn papers, knowing full well that when he left the ranch once more, he would lose his rights, would lose his ace in the hole for all time.

The idea filled him with a feeling of loss he couldn't explain.

But no one would expect any different from him. Despite the fact that the years had matured him, that he'd found a steady niche for himself on the rodeo circuit, that he'd even managed to fatten his bank account probably more than either of his older brothers had managed to do, Chance knew that he would have a knee-jerk reaction to his father and brothers' condescending attitudes and meet their low expectations, just as he always did.

And the same with Pru's expectations, he thought with real regret, not having been able to put the redhead out of his mind.

Some nights she'd been all he could think about. Some days, he'd been hard-pressed not to ride straight for Silver Springs and her. Only the more he'd thought about doing so, the more he'd resisted. Now here he was, practically spitting distance from the one woman he couldn't get out of his system, and he wasn't doing a damned thing about it. And he didn't even know why.

*Oh, yes, you do,* a devilish voice argued. *What if she hasn't stuck around? What if some other man came in while you were gone and claimed her?*

The thought made his gut tie up tight, but he wouldn't believe it. Pru wouldn't go to another man, not when she loved *him.* And she'd always welcomed him back with open arms.

*But even a woman besotted won't wait forever,* the devil argued.

And he *had* been gone longer than ever—

Chance bit back the uncertainty. Pru would be here, he told himself, and he'd face her soon, but first things first.

First, he had to let the old man know he'd arrived.

Taking a deep breath, Chance hopped back in his truck and headed for the place he'd never quite thought of as his real home…and the inevitable confrontation awaiting him.

ALL QUIET. Everyone gone off to wherever. He could do as he pleased.

Emmett Quarrels stepped out of the ranch house into the crisp fall air and strutted across the yard to the supply shed. The middle of the day—Barton and the boys were moving cows, his grandkids were in school and his housekeeper, Felice, had gone to visit her sister over in Taos.

Hallelujah, he was a free man for a few hours, at least!

He hadn't been able to get around the place the way he'd wanted for weeks—not since Barton and the kids had arrived from Albuquerque to settle in. Always a set of eyes watching him, waiting for him to show signs of dying.

Well, he wasn't dead yet.

And even though he'd turned the Curly-Q into a family corporation, even though he'd lured Barton from his lawman job with promises that he could run the place, Emmett wasn't about to take his finger off the spread's pulse. Not when he was still the heart of the Curly-Q, which *he'd* built into one of the biggest ranches in the area.

His three sons had all deserted their heritage years ago. Oh, Chance kept coming back, but never for long enough that it mattered. Emmett never had been able to count on his youngest son for anything, not any more than he'd been able to count on Chance's mother, who one day had picked up and walked away from them all and had never looked back.

For a time, Emmett remembered with satisfaction, he'd gotten along well enough without his boys. But the economy had gone sour, and by the time the country had started righting itself, his luck had gone south…albeit with help.

But he wouldn't think about that now. Wouldn't depress himself with what had been going wrong around the ranch just when things were starting to look up. Barton would make sure things went right from now on. And he himself had work to do and an appetite to prove that he was still the same man he had always been.

Emmett headed for the supply shed to take inventory and soon lost himself in taking stock. Not that he was where he wanted to be—back on a horse.

But for now, anything that made him feel connected, useful, would do. He'd be riding range soon enough if he had his way, but he didn't want to queer the deal. Everything had to be in place, nice and neat, according to plan.

So he got busy, soon found himself at the business end of a ladder.

Engrossed, he was so startled when the door banged open that he nearly fell from a considerable height.

"Lookin' to kill yourself the quick way, Pa?"

Emmett froze, then pulled himself together and turned to look down on his youngest son, who never failed to remind him of the irresponsible woman Chance's mother had been.

He cleared his throat and gruffly said, "So you got here all right." Ever so casually he descended, forcing himself to keep it nice and slow. He had to play this right or he'd ruin everything.

"Did you think I wouldn't show after signing your papers?" Chance asked.

Emmett fought the urge to throw his arm around his youngest son's shoulders. "I never know with you, Boy, now do I?"

"No, you never do." Jaw tight, Chance gave him a measuring look. "What're you doing up on a ladder, anyhow?"

Unable to keep the hostility from his voice, Emmett grumbled, "What do you think—I was looking for something."

"And no one else could do it for you?"

"No one else around." Even if he had set himself up for it, Emmett hated being treated as though he couldn't pull on his own pants.

"I'm here now." Chance stepped toward the ladder. "What is it you need?"

"It can wait for Moon-Eye."

The boy stopped in his tracks. "Right. I can't even be trusted with finding something for you," he muttered.

"Never mind that now." Hoping to avoid an argument, Emmett moved to the door. "Let's go back to the house, get us a cup of coffee and some of Felice's homemade cinnamon rolls." His son had always been a sucker for them.

"Coffee?" Right behind him, Chance said, "And you with a heart condition?"

"I meant decaf," Emmett grumbled.

Felice would threaten to pin back his ears if she ever caught him drinking the real stuff.

Not that he would ever take orders from *any* woman.

But he was willing to give on things that didn't matter if only to placate his housekeeper. Felice had been around longer than all three of his wives put together, and he didn't want to break in a new employee. Besides, if she were gone...well, he'd miss the way she managed things.

"You're awfully concerned about my health all of a sudden," Emmett said.

"I heard you were dying."

"Disappointed that I'm not at death's door yet?"

A weird expression crossed Chance's features so like his mother's. "I would never wish anyone dead, Pa..."

*Not even you* hung between them unspoken.

At least Emmett imagined it did.

His relationships with all his sons left something to be desired, but the one with Chance had always been the most complicated...and maybe the hardest on them both. He'd been crazy in love with the boy's mother and had thought Sunny'd felt the same about him until she'd run away. And Chance was so much like his mother...

Emmett guessed he'd always leaned on the boy harder than he had on Barton or Reed. Then again, his youngest had always needed a firmer hand, Emmett reminded himself. Not that a firm hand had ever seemed to do any good.

On the way back to the house, Emmett came face-to-face with Chance's truck, whose brilliant blue finish shone even through the red dust coating it.

"Well, well, a real Cowboy Cadillac. Must've set you back some," Emmett muttered, checking out the load in back, as well. In addition to his son's clothing bag, there was gear—two bronc saddles and assorted leathers plus a couple of pairs of chaps. But the big-ticket item was a motorcycle that looked brand-new. "I didn't know day workers got paid so well."

"I haven't done day work for several years now. But I'm sure you know that, since your lawyer tracked me down at the rodeo grounds."

"Speaking of rodeo, one of your old bronc-bustin' buddies came this way looking to say howdy a few weeks back, and Bart hired him."

"Who would that be?"

"Name's Will Spencer."

"Billy-Boy Spencer?" Chance mused. "Haven't seem him in some time. He got busted up pretty badly—Fourth of July, I think it was. Took him out of competition for the season."

"Well, he sits a horse real good now."

"Obviously not good enough to rodeo."

"Why do you assume that?" Emmett asked. "Maybe he's just tired of drifting, wants to settle someplace—"

Chance snorted. "Yeah, that's it, Pa. Will wants to make his fortune as a hired hand."

"So you're saying rodeoing is more profitable than cowboying these days?"

"It is if you're good. And it's a lot easier way to make a decent living, that's for sure."

"Always the easy way for you." Emmett ignored the stony glare as he took a closer look at the shiny motorcycle planted in the bed of the truck. "Planning on using this to round up cattle?"

"Does it look like a dirt bike?"

"No. *That* would be useful," Emmett muttered as Chance grabbed his bags.

"You know, I think I'll skip that coffee and take me a lie-down." He started for the house.

"Forgot to tell you Lainey has your old room. I had to give Barton the whole wing for his family."

Chance stopped dead in his tracks and turned. A fleeting expression crossed the boy's features—Emmett would swear it was hurt—before his face went blank.

"Of course you did," Chance said evenly, but Emmett heard something darker behind the calm words. "So where *do* I stay? The bunkhouse?"

"Temporarily." And even as his son shifted direction, started off for the building that at the moment housed only two hired hands, he quickly said, "But you'll eat with the family up at the house."

Chance wouldn't need anything more, anyway, Emmett assured himself. His son's whole life revolved around trading one temporary situation for another.

"Hey, Pa," Chance called over his shoulder as he stalked away. "Good to see you, too."

Silently watching until Chance slammed into the bunkhouse, Emmett was duly shamed that he hadn't even welcomed his youngest son home.

THE BUNKHOUSE had two bunk rooms—one on either side of a common area that served as living and dining room. And on the other side of an alcove that served as a miniature kitchen was a common bathroom.

Chance actually remembered the days when the bunkhouse was bustling with men. Maybe not eight of them—the most the place could hold—but five or six, anyhow.

One of the bunk rooms seemed to be in use by two men—Will and whoever else his father or brother had hired. So Billy-Boy Spencer was here, Chance mused. While they were acquainted from the rodeo circuit, had shared a beer a few times, Chance wouldn't say they were buddies.

He wondered whose interpretation of their acquaintanceship that had been—Will's or Pa's? That comment of Pa's about Will maybe giving up drifting—that had been aimed at *him,* of that he was certain.

The second bedroom remained empty and neglected. Two sets of double bunks set against opposite walls, and loose sheets covered all four mattresses to keep off the dust. But Chance liked being alone, so he didn't mind. He threw his gear down near an old beat-up bureau and pulled the sheet from one of the lower bunks.

A small cloud of fine particles whirled around him.

"Welcome home, Chance," he muttered. "Good to see you, Son. I'm right proud you decided to go in on the deal with your brothers and me." Chance laughed bitterly. "Yeah, right. I'll hear *those* words…never."

As if the old man would ever make him feel like more than some interloper. He should have known. Probably the only reason his father had included him on the deal was so that Chance wouldn't have a legal leg to stand on if he tried to claim some inheritance later.

"Don't worry, Pa, I won't be troubling you for long."

He didn't need any damn inheritance. He had enough money stashed away to make a down payment on a little spread of his own.

*If* he ever decided he wanted one.

More unsettled than when he'd started out, Chance felt as if he could use a fast ride to cool off. And not one on a horse, either. Thinking about rounding up Pru, getting her on the back of his motorcycle, arms wrapped around his waist, head pressed against his back, decided him.

He washed up quickly and changed into one of his fancy dress shirts that Pru liked so well—the back was decorated with a mustang racing across a sunset—and slicked back his long hair, tying it at his neck with a leather thong.

Hearing a vehicle, he figured someone had arrived—probably Saint Bart.

He set a pair of sunglasses on his face, pulled his hat low over his forehead and stepped out of the bunkhouse, only to be met with a startling sight.

Inspecting his truck and bike was a slender six-footer with dark hair who looked exactly like Bart had at sixteen. Feeling as if he'd just whipped back in time two whole decades, Chance realized he was staring at his nephew, who had managed to grow up since the last time they saw each other a couple of Christmases back.

"Daniel!" he called. "That is *you,* right?"

The teenager grinned and rushed him. "Uncle Chance! You came! Wait until Dad hears!"

No doubt Bart had told his son that his irresponsible uncle would never show.

Staring past a colorfully blooming bruise under one of his nephew's bright blue eyes and taking in the rugged, still-developing features so like Bart's, Chance was at a loss as to how to greet the teenager now that he was no longer a kid.

But Daniel didn't hesitate. He threw his arms around his uncle and pounded him on the back in a manly fashion. Feeling welcomed at last, Chance reciprocated. Then uncle and nephew stepped apart, both grinning and snorting with a fleeting embarrassment.

"So, where did you get that shiner?" Chance finally asked, giving it a better look.

Daniel grinned. "At school. That's why I'm home early. The principle doesn't want to see my face for the rest of the week. Man, Dad's gonna kill me."

Chance refrained from commenting, but *like father like son* sprang to mind. When Bart had been the new kid at school, he'd come home with a few bruises and split lips of his own. Still, knowing his judgmental brother, who viewed everything in black-and-white—undoubtedly a prerequisite for being a lawman—Chance figured the teenager *would* be in trouble.

"So your dad doesn't know," Chance mused. "Then how'd you get home?"

As Daniel said, "Felice came and got me," the housekeeper herself flew out the door.

"Chance...my Chance!" Felice yelled excitedly as she hurried into his waiting arms. "You're home at last!"

Grinning, Chance spun Felice around, allowing her

to hug and kiss him all she wanted, then squeezed her so hard that she smacked him in the chest so he would release her.

"These bones are getting too old for your shenanigans," she complained, a wide smile nevertheless pulling at her mouth.

Chance smiled back. "You're what now? All of forty?"

Her still-smooth olive skin flushed as she threw back her head and laughed at their ongoing joke about her age. In reality, she was past sixty, but with only a few silver threads in her dark hair and fewer permanent laugh lines around her dark eyes, she did look much younger.

Felice said, "You silver-tongued devil."

"You doubt my sincerity?" He feigned hurt.

All part of their affectionate game...

Felice Cuma had been housekeeper to his father forever—ever since Chance could remember. And she'd been the closest thing to a mother he'd ever known. His biological mother having abandoned him when he was a toddler, Felice had taken care of all his needs, had dressed his scrapes and kissed away his hurts and had defended him against his older brothers and father when they'd gotten down on him.

Chance had always wished Felice *was* his biological mother. As a small child, he used to pretend and had even called her Mama for a while, no matter that she tried to make him stop. Then Pa had overheard one too many times and had grown furious. His threat to punish Chance if he kept it up had finally put an end to the childish fantasy forever.

Felice had always tried to make him believe that the Curly-Q was his home, though, and in truth, she was the main reason he'd kept coming back...until he'd gotten involved with Pru, that was.

As if the mother of his heart could read his mind, Felice eyed him and brushed an imaginary speck of dust off his shoulder. "You're off to find Pru?"

"You know me too well."

"Better than you know her."

His heart stilled before it started to pump double time. "What?" he asked lightly, attempting to hide his deepest fear. "She's not in Silver Springs?"

"Oh, she's here, at Justine's."

"Then what's the problem?" Something about her manner convinced him there was one. "There isn't..."

The words *another man* stuck in his throat.

"You! You're the problem. Gone for more than two years— Chance, what were you thinking? What do you expect from a woman?"

"Nothing," he said, though he was trying to convince himself.

"Then nothing is what you'll get." She shook her head. "Go see her, find out for yourself."

Properly chastised, now unsure of his reception, Chance thought maybe he ought to wait a while longer....

Now he *really* needed that ride.

Daniel happily helped him get the motorcycle off the truck and enthused over the machine so much that Chance agreed to let his nephew try it out later.

As Chance shot away from the ranch buildings accompanied by the band of horses that hung around the house as if to act as escort to incoming and outgoing vehicles, he was thinking that Daniel and his little sister Lainey were the best part of his brother.

He wondered if Bart had proper appreciation for that fact.

And whenever he was around those two great kids, Chance also got to wondering what it might be like to have a small brood of his own.

Which kick started more thoughts about Pru…

Her dark-red hair begging for his fingers to tangle in the curls. Her lush body begging to be held and stroked to the brink of ecstasy and back. Her big hazel eyes begging him to love her again and again.

But it wasn't just the physical that made him long for this particular woman.

It was how she made him laugh. How she managed to frustrate and intrigue him. How she made him feel different about himself when he was with her.

Chance tried resisting the ache growing inside him to see her, but in the end, as if it had a will of its own, his motorcycle shot straight through the sagging, half-deserted town of Silver Springs and headed onto a narrow back road. The Garner place sat a half mile from the home-and-feed store that Mitch had taken over when his father had retired.

And, as if she knew he was coming for her, Pru was outside the house, sitting on the board and rope swing her brother-in-law had put together for his girls, one of whom happened to be perched on her lap. A brief smile crossed his lips as he took in the blazing orange shirt that clashed with the dark-red curls trailing her shoulders.

Typical Pru style.

Then Chance acknowledged the tightening of his gut as, once more, he rode back into the preacher's daughter's life.

# Chapter Two

As a motorcycle roared behind them, Pru's grasp on Hope tightened. She didn't have to turn around to see that it was Chance Quarrels. She just knew.

The engine died too close for comfort.

Trying not to panic, she kissed her daughter's cheek and whispered, "Honey, go play with Blythe and Fancy," set Hope down and watched her toddle over to join her cousins.

Still Pru didn't turn around, and she now felt Chance behind her. Heart thudding, she braced herself for denials, should they become necessary.

But when he said, "So Mitch and Justine had themselves another little girl, huh? I hadn't heard," the invisible fist clenching her stomach eased a bit.

Back still to him, she murmured, "You haven't been around to hear anything for a long while, have you?"

Relief that he didn't recognize Hope as his daughter warred with disappointment—a familiar emotion Chance had stirred in her for more years than she wanted to acknowledge.

"I'm here now, Pru."

Heart thudding, she finally turned. Her gaze

quickly devoured Chance, though his golden brown hair was tied back at the base of his neck, his handsome, tanned face was shadowed by a white Stetson, and his glowing blue eyes were hidden behind sunglasses. She didn't have to connect with them to see them in her mind's eye.

And she didn't have to sweep her gaze over his six-foot-plus, rangy body to remember every inch of it—the long, corded neck, shoulders and arms well muscled without being pumped, stomach as hard as a washboard, long, lean legs and a tight butt that had drawn more admiring glances from other women than she'd cared to recognize.

As he always had, Chance stirred something essential deep inside her. Only *this* time, she told herself, she *would* ignore it all.

To prove her resolve, Pru arched an eyebrow and asked, ''Am I supposed to be thrilled that you've included Silver Springs in your busy itinerary?''

His lips curled into an easy smile. ''I was hoping you'd be a *little* glad to see me.''

''And how long would that be for this time?'' she asked, keeping her tone wry and a bit distant.

He didn't answer. Not that she thought he really would. He stared at her for a moment longer. His gaze pierced those sunglasses and set the air between them afire.

Then, in his most seductive tone, he murmured, ''I missed you, Miss Prudence.''

A thrill shot through Pru, and she mentally cursed her own weakness. The only time he ever called her that was when he made love to her.

Fighting the urge to melt right down into her boots, she drawled, ''I could tell you were just pining

away for me. All those phone calls…and the post-
cards and letters…why, all that attention was powerful overwhelming.''

"No need to get snippy, Prudence Prescott, when
you know that's not my style.''

"What *is* your style, Chance Quarrels?'' Pru
asked, finally losing the hold on her temper. "What
kind of a man tells a woman he loves her only to
leave town without so much as a by-your-leave?''

"Why don't we talk about it away from here. I
thought we could take a ride on my new bike—''

She cut him off. "Well, think again. I'm not going
anywhere with you.''

"You're ticked at me.''

"No, Chance, not ticked. Not hardly. Not anymore. I don't even know that's how I felt two years
ago when you just up and disappeared again without
a word. I was disappointed, yes. And a little sad.''
Heartbroken was more like it…not that she would
say it. "Now, I just don't feel much of anything.''
A bold-faced lie, but she thought she uttered it convincingly enough.

His expression changed slightly as if maybe he
believed her. "But you're not *with* anyone else,
right?'' His stance shifted, making him appear to be
unsure of himself.

Grasping that as a weapon she could use if she so
chose, Pru said, "That would be none of your business anymore.''

As if to punctuate the finality of that statement,
angry little-girl shrieks whipped her gaze away from
the man who was an addiction to her.

Blythe's fingers were tangled in Fancy's red curls.
A furious Fancy shoved Blythe, who flew backward,

outstretched arm catching toddler Hope and knocking her over. The two sisters continued their battle, and a yard away Hope sat on the ground screaming indignantly.

"Girls, stop it right now!" Pru yelled as she raced toward them. She couldn't believe they were acting up like this with Chance around. She didn't want him to so much as notice Hope. "Fancy! Blythe!"

Trying to decide which to do first—pick up her unharmed yet frightened daughter to comfort her or separate her two hellion nieces before one of them drew blood—Pru hesitated a second too long.

Chance whipped by her and scooped Hope up into his arms, saying, "I've got the little one—"

"Her name's Hope and you give her to me!" Pru gasped, frantic that he would look into their daughter's eyes and *know* as Justine had suggested.

"Hold on, I'm not gonna drop her or anything. Someone's got to do something about them—" he indicated her nieces "—but I'm not one to get between two fighting females. And *you* can't break up that fight if your arms are full," he reasoned, settling his daughter against his hip as if it were the most natural thing in the world.

Throat tight with misgivings, Pru nodded and turned to the two little girls, who were still screeching and flailing at each other. She towered over them and said between clenched teeth, "If you two don't stop right now, I'm going to give you the longest time-out of your lives!"

That got through to the little hoydens. With a last poke from Blythe and a halfhearted shove from Fancy, they stepped apart, both pouting and sniffling.

"I'm ashamed of you two. You're sisters. How

could you try to hurt each other?'' Pru demanded, all the while remembering how many times she and Justine had given each other bruises and scrapes. History repeating itself.

"She started it!" Blythe whined.

"Did not!"

"Enough!" Pru yelled. "Now go to your room and wait on your beds quietly for me."

"Yes, Aunt Pru," they said in one voice.

But they weren't of one mind as they stomped back to the house, making faces and sticking out tongues at each other.

"No more hitting!" Pru warned.

Then, a sense of dread gripping her, she turned to face the quiet behind her. For a moment she stood stock-still and speechless as she took in a sight she'd been both longing and dreading to see for nearly two years now—Chance engaged by their daughter and vice versa.

They looked so natural together, Pru realized. Hope fit into the crook of her daddy's arm as if it were made to hold only her. One little foot kicked his stomach, but if he noticed, he didn't seem to mind. Chance was grinning at the toddler, charming her.

Pru wanted to rush in and grab her precious daughter, wrap her arms around her and protect her from the man who could break her tiny heart. Instead, she stood frozen, unable—unwilling, even—to end the moment. Tears stung the backs of her eyelids and a longing, so deep she couldn't even put words to it, whipped through her.

Chance made a silly face at his daughter. Hope giggled and grabbed for his sunglasses. She got them halfway down his nose before he caught her tiny hand in his.

"No, you don't, Squirt."

He stared over the rim of the sunglasses straight into Hope's eyes. Pru's breath caught in her throat. *Now he would know!* When Chance winked, Hope threw back her head and shrilled with laughter.

Which somehow broke the spell.

"Her name is Hope, not Squirt," Pru muttered, stepping toward them, holding out her arms for her child and gearing herself up for any necessary denials.

"M'ma!" Hope squealed.

Pru's stomach knotted, and her voice was thick as she said, "Chance, give her over."

Chubby arms reaching for her, Hope repeated the demand. "M'ma!"

Pru snatched her precious child from the man who seemed to have no clue that he'd sired her, as he asked, "What's that she's saying?"

Panicking, Pru said the first thing that came to her.

"She's hungry." Grasping at straws to keep the truth from Chance, she turned the small lie into a whopper. "Whenever Hope gets *really* hungry, she makes that weird little sound."

"Oh."

"So I'd better feed her and talk to her cou—" Catching herself before she blew it, Pru covered by clearing her throat and saying, "Um, I need to get in there and talk to Fancy and Blythe."

Not seeming to notice her near blunder, Chance mused, "She looks just like her mother, doesn't she?"

Pru's heart skipped a beat. "Wh-what?"

"Squirt here—she has Justine's nose and lips."

Which happened to be Pru's nose and lips, as well. She and Justine had always looked a lot alike. She ought to be thankful for small favors.

*Ought to...*

"M'ma!" Hope sang, curling her fingers in Pru's hair and putting her baby cheek to Pru's.

Knees weak, kissing the soft skin, Pru wished she could think them inside, instantly away from the man who had such a disastrous effect on her. Around him, she needed all her wits, impossible in this situation.

Time to extricate herself.

"Okay, sweetheart, I'll get you something to eat." She patted the toddler's back, then said to Chance, "She's *real* hungry. And like I said, I've got to take care of the girls. Justine's at the store with Mitch this afternoon. So I have to get. That means," she said pointedly, when he didn't budge, "that *you* get, too."

Sunglasses back in place so she couldn't see his eyes, Chance shrugged, maybe a bit too casually. "All right. For now."

"For *good* would be better."

"You don't mean that."

"How would you know?"

"I know you."

Too well, Pru feared, her desire to see him gone being half-hearted. But unwilling to give him the edge, she sweetly asked, "Do you?"

A staring contest ensued. Rather, Pru gave him her infamous evil eye while he seemed to be studying her benignly in return. Double damnation! How could she tell *what* he was thinking behind those dark glasses?

Without breaking the connection, Chance slowly backed up. "I'll catch you later, then."

The promise made her stomach flutter, but she coolly said, "Don't bother. You'll just be wasting your time."

"We'll see, Prunella."

"And don't call me that ridiculous name."

"Not ridiculous. Cute." Out popped that smile that made her pulse jump and her knees weak. "And if I remember correctly, you used to think it was cute, too."

"Never."

"Liar," he murmured.

Pru didn't argue the point, and neither did Chance. They seemed to be at a standoff, still staring at each other. Someone had to give first. Normally, that wouldn't be her, but Pru had Hope to consider.

She turned away, murmuring, "C'mon sweetheart, let's get you inside."

Away from the father who hadn't recognized his own daughter, even though he'd gazed into eyes identical to his own. Justine had been all wet on that one!

And so had she...

As much as she'd wanted to keep Hope's identity from Chance, she had thought he would recognize his own flesh and blood. And Pru hadn't realized how torn she would be when she saw him again. She'd thought she had it all sorted out in her mind. Chance would be bad for Hope just as he was bad for *her*.

But seeing them together had given her a jolt. A big dose of reality she had wanted to ignore. She'd been filled with a longing for something that would never be.

Chance was Chance, she reminded herself, and he'd always counted on her to be waiting for him with open arms. Not that he alone was to blame. She'd liked the exciting relationship, which had suited her unconventional nature.

Or at least she had at the beginning.

But now she didn't have just herself to think of. She couldn't run off on a whim and do whatever she felt like doing as she had the first twenty-five years of her life. Now she had responsibilities, something Chance had always managed to avoid. She was just going to have to stay away from him, Pru realized. It was the only way....

Still, once inside the house, she couldn't help herself. Hope balanced on her hip, babbling in a language only the two of them shared, Pru watched through the kitchen window until Chance sped away on his new motorcycle, disappearing down the road like an already-fading memory.

UNSETTLED BY PRU'S reaction to him, Chance rode, the memory of her scent still with him, until the bike was nearly out of gas. Once refueled, he headed back to the Curly-Q.

He'd expected some resistance after such a long absence—she wouldn't have been Pru if she hadn't given him a hard time—but he'd also expected to charm her into giving over, at least a little. Only this time charm hadn't worked. Apparently, she wasn't celebrating his return, and once again he worried that she might have found someone else. The possibility tied him up in knots that no stretch of road could ease.

He'd been wrong, staying away for so long. He guessed he would have to admit that to her. It was the best he had, but would his best be good enough?

This love thing he didn't understand, didn't know that he wanted to. He'd rather ride a dozen wild bulls than have to think about his emotions long enough to make sense of them. What he did understand was that having Pru back in his life was absolutely essential to his mental well-being, especially now.

Now, more than ever, he needed her to argue with him, to tease him into a good mood, to make love with him. Make him feel whole again.

He understood something else, as well—his showing up had made Pru unbearably uncomfortable, proving that she wasn't immune to him yet.

He guessed that was a start.

She needed time, he told himself. She would come around. All he had to do was to be his usual charming self. And patient.

But what about when he left again—what would that do to her? his conscience asked. Obviously, she hadn't taken it too well this last time.

And he *would* be leaving. Soon.

Guilt rode him down into the canyon. Not that his leaving would be altogether his decision this time— he would have to go, and he didn't know how long he'd have to be away. Not his choice. Not his fault.

*His fault...*

Even as the words echoed in his head, another guilt surfaced, and the slain man rose to haunt him. Rather the photo of Julio Alvarez and his wife and five kids—he'd seen it on the news enough. Not that he'd ever met the security guard. Nor could he have guessed at this tragedy. But justification wouldn't bring the poor bastard back.

*His fault…*

Down on the canyon floor, escorted by the small band of loose horses and the ranch dogs, he roared right up to the bunkhouse and parked his motorcycle next to the building. Then he bent over and patted A.C. and D.C., who apparently still remembered him, though they'd been little more than pups when he'd last been on the Curly-Q.

That the dogs were hanging around the buildings meant the men had returned from the range for the day. Odd, considering how early it was. The sun was low in the sky but hadn't yet set. The men should be packing in every second of daylight on the range.

He waited outside for a minute, expecting some-one new to straggle out of the main house to greet him. His big brother, Bart, for example.

But either no one noticed his return or no one cared—the more likely of the two—so he went in-side, yelling, "Anyone home?" hoping he'd get a chance to say hi to Will.

The fading smell of food still permeated the main room, but he got no answer.

Whoever had been there was gone now.

Someone had been in his bunk room, as well, Chance realized the moment he entered. Since all signs of dust had been removed, he had no doubt that it had been Felice. She was still taking care of him. He'd have to give her an extra-big hug when he went over to the main house for supper.

Grinning at the thought of making her squeal at him, he decided to finish unpacking before heading over. Earlier, he'd just pulled what he'd needed from one of his bags. Now he took the time to hang his fancy shirts and jeans in the big wardrobe, making sure to snap the wrinkles out first. Next he opened one of the empty bureau drawers.

From the second bag, he scooped up myriad socks, briefs and undershirts and shoved them inside, then took a moment to neaten them up just in case Felice took it in mind to do it for him.

Dipping his hand into the bag again, this time to gather a couple of bandannas, Chance frowned when his fingers hit something other than cotton. He spread the mouth of the bag and took a better look inside— then went after the pale item that glowed up at him.

For a moment, he stared at the blank envelope— one that he'd never before seen. His breath thickened, and a warning twinge tightened his gut.

The envelope wasn't empty.

An undefined wariness washed through him, but he quickly put any conjectures on hold. He ripped one end from the envelope and shook free the contents. A single sheet of paper floated loose and landed on his bunk, looking every bit as dangerous as a rattler.

He treated it as such as he picked up the paper gingerly between forefinger and thumb, while questions roared through his head.

Who the hell had gotten into his bag?

And when?

Only a third question could be answered at the moment, and that by reading the missive to learn its contents…as if he couldn't guess. He unfolded the sheet and silently read the note printed in a neat hand, which he didn't recognize.

Evoking the Cowboy Code
by the Cowboy Poet

The Cowboy Code is old and strong—
you need to abide by it to get along.
Those who don't find themselves alone—
and more often than not, in the danger zone.
Get the message?

Chance's jaw tightened, and his gaze narrowed.

He got the drift, all right. No matter how prettily phrased, this was a blatant warning. But from whom? Obviously someone fancied himself a poet—and he knew dozens of cowboys who would qualify, especially when they'd had a few drinks too many.

Equally important, Chance wanted to know how the missive had found its way into his bag.

He thought it through.

He'd packed the day before. Someone could have picked the lock to his hotel room and deposited the envelope there. Or it could have happened while he'd been having breakfast that morning. The bags had lain in the back of his pickup—anyone could have gotten to them.

Reading the grim piece of poetry again, he shook his head at his own predicament.

He wasn't in an easy position, that was for damn sure. He wasn't even surprised by the warning—he'd been getting cold shoulders from people and hearing subtle threats for too long. Having felt the heat for several weeks now had helped him decide to wait it out here at the ranch.

How seriously should he take this warning? Chance wondered. And was it just that? Someone angry enough to speak out over his turning against his own kind? Or was there more—a seriousness that he'd best not ignore?

If the Cowboy Poet knew where he'd headed, trouble might very well have followed him.

Chance shook off the weird feeling that gave him. Probably all smoke anyhow, he tried to tell himself. Even so, he'd be sure to watch out for his back. If he needed to, he could always disappear ahead of schedule.

Except...

He didn't want to disappear. Not yet. Not until he'd held Pru in his arms at least one more time.

Only...

He didn't want to love Pru and leave her again, either.

That was the damnable part about coming back to Silver Springs and the Curly-Q—he didn't know *what* he wanted.

Frustration drove him from his isolation. The notion of sharing his predicament with Bart uppermost in his mind—surely his lawman brother might have some thoughts on how to deal with the matter—he decided to head for the main house for a little soul baring.

He left the bunkhouse just as Moon-Eye Hobb was about to enter his quarters. Liking his privacy, unwilling to climb on the back of a horse, the old hand hadn't liked living in the bunkhouse with the *real* cowboys. So he'd built himself a room and bath at one end of the long supply shed years ago. Chance had been a teenager then and had helped the old hand install the plumbing.

"Hey, Moon-Eye, have I really been gone so long you don't even recognize me?" he called.

Old and grizzled, average in height, but square in stature, Moon-Eye gave Chance the once-over with his good eye. His left eyelid was only half-open, and no iris was visible—only part of a milky-white eyeball.

"Chance!" Moon-Eye strode away from the building and met Chance halfway, where he gave him a hearty slap on the back. "Good to see you, boy!"

"You, too, you old buzzard," Chance said with affection. "Hey, what's going on around here? If we're so hard-pressed to get those calves to market, why is everyone in so early?"

"We got problems, Chance." Moon-Eye shook his head. "The Curly-Q's got big prob—" The ring of a telephone from inside his room interrupted. "Listen, I got to get that call. Let's catch up later, after dinner."

"If I'm around."

"Pru, huh?" The phone rang again, and Moon-Eye backed away from Chance. "Tomorrow, then. Good to see you, boy," he said again, then whipped around and limped as fast as he could toward his private quarters.

Leaving Chance wondering what it was, exactly, that Pa hadn't told him.

## Chapter Three

Chance entered without announcing himself. Delicious hints of supper and a conversation between Felice and an unfamiliar female too mature to be his niece Lainey wafted from the kitchen. He got an earful of what sounded like a cooking lesson.

Moon-Eye's words in mind, he veered toward the wing where the old man had his office in addition to his bedroom. The door stood open and he heard a familiar male voice.

"But you're pretty sure Frank's gonna recover 100 percent, right?" his brother was saying.

Drawing closer, Chance saw Bart was on the telephone, worry pulling at the rugged features that kept him from being exactly handsome. Nevertheless, Chance could remember when all the local girls were hot for Bart. He'd always attributed it to the aura of power and authority that his brother carried around in that big body and bigger attitude of his.

Just like Pa used to.

But Pa had changed some, grown smaller for one. He'd shrunk into a husk of his former self to Chance's mind. At the moment, however, Chance was reminded of the way he'd been once. Gaze narrowed, expression grim and determined, Pa sat forward, elbows hooked on his desk, obviously intent on Bart's conversation—the difference being that he was listening for once rather than orchestrating things.

"Uh-huh. Well, thanks, Doc," Bart was saying. "I'll give you a call later to get an update." He replaced the receiver in its cradle.

"Frank's all right, then?"

"The doctor thinks he'll be right as rain, but he wants to keep Frank overnight to monitor him since he did lose consciousness. And he said to give the guy a couple of days off until his arm heals."

"Thank God it wasn't any worse."

What the hell was going on? Chance wondered, surprised that neither man even noticed him as he lounged in the doorway.

"Pa, I'm not sure this was an accident," Bart said. "You wouldn't have any idea—"

"Of course I wouldn't!"

"Well, something's not right around here and hasn't been since before—"

Chance cleared his throat and stepped into the room, figuring that if he didn't announce himself, no one would recognize the fact that he was there.

As Bart turned, annoyance crossed his features. "Back from gallivanting around, are you?"

Chance didn't skip a beat. "Good to see you, too, Bart. It's been what? Nearly three years?"

"I didn't think you kept track of these things."

Concerned about the conversation he'd overheard added to Moon-Eye's dire warning, Chance ignored the dig. "So what did I interrupt?"

"One of the hands, Frank Ewing, got himself hurt today," Emmett said.

Chance looked to his brother. "I heard you say you didn't think it was an accident. What happened?"

"A whole line of fence in the south pasture was down, and the cows already started migrating where we didn't want 'em. Looked like someone had rammed the posts with a truck—they snapped off near the base like twigs."

"You're right. That *doesn't* sound like an accident," Chance said, "though it could have been a drunk cowboy blowing off payday steam."

"Could've, but I don't think so," Bart said darkly. "Moon-Eye and Frank went out there this afternoon with the post-hole digger to do repairs. Seems like someone might've messed with the equipment, too. Frank was lucky he didn't lose an arm, and his passing out was a little bonus that scared the stuffing out of old Moon-Eye."

"You think someone purposely tried to maim him?"

"Not him specifically. Maybe not any man," Bart said. "But cause us costly delays? You bet."

Chance looked from Bart to their father. "What the hell's going on around here?"

"That's what I've been trying to figure out for weeks," Bart admitted.

"There's more?"

"You betcha—a whole slew of bad-luck incidents, ranging from an unexpected outbreak of anthrax to a broken windmill and lots more in between. Incidents that have drained the Curly-Q of funds to the point that the mortgage is going begging." Bart turned an intense and suspicious gaze on the old man. "Right, Pa?"

"Don't look at me like that," Emmett blustered. "Every ranch hits a bad-luck streak sometime. If I knew anything different, don't you think I'd tell you?"

"Maybe…depending on how it would affect your plans," Chance said, gratified when Bart gave him a surprised look. Obviously they could agree on something.

"You give me more credit than I deserve," their father groused.

"I don't know, Pa," Bart said, humor bleeding through his serious demeanor. "I'd say you pretty much deserve everything you get."

"I hope the two of you are having a good time picking on a sick old man who can't even defend himself."

Chance's grin dried up, and he noticed Bart sobered, as well. Then, with an expression that seemed a bit too self-satisfied, Pa picked himself up from behind the desk and stalked out of the room, muttering something under his breath. The only thing Chance actually caught was his and Bart's names. He stared openmouthed at his father's retreating back.

When the old man disappeared from sight, Chance mused, "He's using that heart condition of his like a weapon on us."

"You already noticed, and you haven't even been around twenty-four hours yet. Took me a little longer to sort it out."

Chance shrugged. "My powers of observation are as good as they've ever been."

"Everything else about you the same, too?" Bart asked. "Or are we in for a surprise?"

A criticism if Chance had ever heard one. "Yeah, I'm still the same good-for-nothing kid you used to rag on," he said just as Bart no doubt expected.

"Only when you deserved it."

"Which was always?" Chance had a long memory and he tended to nurse old grudges—he'd never forgotten one mean thing his brother and father had said to or about him. "Don't get on any high horse with me, Saint Bart. You weren't the model of perfection Pa made you out to be. You just happened to hold the title."

"What title would that be?"

"Of being the oldest. But that's pretty common, if you ask me—comes one to a family."

"Maybe there was more to the way Pa treated me," Bart suggested. "He recognized my sense of responsibility, for example."

"Yeah, Pa pretty much took that away from Reed and bestowed it upon you the moment you set your coveted boots on Curly-Q soil for good."

Which had happened only after Bart's mother had died. Until then, Bart had only visited a few times a year. And in between, Chance and Reed had been forced to listen to Pa's lament over how his eldest belonged on the Curly-Q…as if *they* didn't. Chance guessed he'd taken the notion to heart. He'd never known how Reed had felt—even then, their middle brother kept everything locked up inside and played with a poker face.

But not so Bart.

At the moment, he appeared more than a little sur-

prised. "Me taking what was Reed's—and yours?—
is that how you see it?"

"No, not how I see it—the truth."

Reed had had certain expectations, especially since
he'd insisted on living on the Curly-Q with Pa rather
than with his own mother after the divorce. Reed had
been the one with the spread until Bart had butted
his way in.

"Well, we all have some uncomfortable truths to
face around here, don't we?"

Bart's drawl and superior expression set Chance's
teeth on edge, and he engaged in yet another staring
match.

What had he been thinking to seek his brother's
advice on anything?

If he told Bart about his predicament, his brother
would place the blame squarely on his shoulders.
Maybe that's where the fault belonged, but Chance
didn't need to hear it from the arrogant ex-lawman,
who never had reason to doubt his own decisions.

Suddenly Chance laughed. "Always set on having
the upper hand, aren't you, Saint Bart?" Taking the
challenge seriously, however, wasn't his style.

"Just playing the hand dealt me…waiting for you
to do the same."

Not willing to let his brother see that what
amounted to criticism bothered him, Chance snorted
and shook his head. "Still the same old Bart."

Bart shrugged. "Back at you."

Their tense exchange having run its course,
Chance could think of nothing more to say, so he
gave his watch exaggerated attention.

"Guess I'd better be on my way."

"You're not staying for supper?"

"Not tonight."

Not after the go-round they'd just had. He wasn't willing to stick his neck out for more, especially not over a dinner table where Pa and Bart could gang up and decorate it with a nasty verbal noose.

"Felice'll be disappointed," Bart said, not hiding his disapproval. "She cooked all your favorites."

"Don't worry, I'll give her my personal appreciation...later. She'll understand why I have to get."

"She'll tolerate it from you, but she won't really understand."

*Something more to feel guilty about.*

Chance's shoulders were feeling burdened by the excess weight. But he'd be damned if he'd stick around to be a psychological punching bag over dinner.

He *would* figure out a way to make it up to Felice, though.

"I suggest you put off your plans until after dinner," Bart suggested.

"Damn, Bart, you're my brother, not my keeper. Don't treat me like one of your kids!"

"Then don't act like one of 'em."

*That did it!*

Jaw clenched, sorry that he'd given his brother the benefit of the doubt for even a moment, Chance fixed his hat lower on his forehead and without another word left the room.

Not back even a day and he was already feeling the urge to ride off into the sunset.

Hopping onto his motorcycle, he did exactly that.

THE SUPPER CROWD was fast filling every table and every counter space at Reba's Café. Most of the pa-

trons were men who worked on local ranches—hired
hands with no one to cook their meals—though the
occasional couple or family showed for a night out.
For the most part, the customers were a goodnatured
lot, and Pru was thankful, because she was having
difficulty keeping her mind on her work tonight.

At one table she forgot to bring the drinks. At
another she brought the wrong order. At a third she
dropped a plate and nearly splattered her customer.

All to her profound embarrassment.

Pru put it down to having been unnerved on her
way to work, when she'd sensed that someone had
been following her at a distance—Chance, no doubt.

She'd expected him to enter the restaurant at any
moment, but so far he remained a no-show.

The owner, Reba Gantry—a good-humored, mid-
dle-aged woman draped in garments that matched the
turquoise adobe walls and purple trim—drifted from
booth to table. Though she always seemed focused
on her patrons, nothing escaped her.

"Pru, honey," Reba said, "why don't you take a
break and pull yourself together before you have a
*real* disaster."

So Pru grabbed some herbal tea and slid into a
booth across from Alcina Dale, owner of Silver
Springs Bed and Breakfast, and a lifelong friend despite the difference in their ages. Nine years older
than she, Alcina used to baby-sit her and Justine
when they were kids.

"I don't know what's wrong with me tonight,"
she muttered, sipping at the nerve-calming tea.

"I could hazard a guess," Alcina said. As usual,
she appeared regal and calm, every inch the together
lady, her pale hair upswept, a string of pearls encas-

ing her elegant neck. "Your mind's on Chance Quarrels. I heard he was back."

With a population of barely more than seventy, news spread like wildfire in Silver Springs.

"Chance didn't even cross my mind," Pru bluffed.

"No, he just has hold of it. He's lurking back there, whether you want him or not."

Pru didn't deny it.

"So did you see him?" Alcina asked.

"He dropped by."

"And…?"

"And I sent him on his way like any self-respecting woman would."

Alcina sighed and pushed the remainder of her food around on her plate. "Sometimes self-respect is overrated."

Pru started at the unexpected sentiment. Alcina was a die-hard feminist with high standards when it came to men. Probably too high. She'd never even had a serious relationship that Pru knew of. Of course, Alcina had been back east at college for all those years…

"You aren't running a fever, are you?" Pru asked.

"I don't mean you shouldn't have self-respect. But sometimes a woman needs more."

"Sometimes a woman can't have what she wants, no matter what."

"Sometimes you have to be honest with a man."

Pru raised both eyebrows. "Like you were with Reed?" She knew all about Alcina's unrequited passion for the middle Quarrels brother.

"That's old history."

"So's Chance."

"Chance is here, seeking you out. Reed never even noticed that I existed."

"Of course he did!"

"Only as his older brother's classmate and friend. You can't compare the two situations."

Alcina was right. Still…

"If I let Chance into my life, he'll just leave it again, and I don't need any more of that."

"Then give him a reason to stay."

Alcina was one of the few people who knew the truth about the identity of Hope's father. But Pru could trust the woman to keep her own counsel.

In a low voice she said, "Look, Alcina, I'm not about to saddle him with responsibility that he doesn't want."

Giving her a searching look, speaking softly as well, Alcina asked, "How can you believe that Chance wouldn't want his own daughter in his life?"

"He *might* want her," Pru acknowledged, "at least until he can't resist wandering off to someplace new."

"That's a possibility, I agree. But are you sure that's the real reason you won't tell him about Hope?"

"You think I'd want him breaking my daughter's heart?"

"Of course not. But I suspect there's more holding you back."

Alcina was too smart to fool, Pru guessed, and had excellent instincts. Pru hadn't told anyone the deeper reason, hadn't even verbalized the logic to herself in so many words until this very minute.

"All right. I want Chance to want *me*," Pru admitted. "But I would never use my child to bind him to me. And if I *did* tell him about Hope and he stayed, I'd never be sure..."

The bells hanging over the door chimed, announcing the arrival of a new customer.

"Well, you have a conundrum there," Alcina said, "because you *are* depriving your child of her father."

So her sister had told her dozens of times, Pru thought wearily. "I just don't see a way out."

"How about being honest with Chance about something else, then," Alcina suggested. "About what you feel for him."

"I already tried that last time."

The blonde's gaze froze at a spot over Pru's left shoulder. Heart skipping a beat, Pru refused to glance back. But a crawly sensation made her slide lower in her booth.

"What?" she whispered, as if she didn't know.

"Speak of the devil..."

Pru wondered how she was supposed to function now, when she was already having trouble keeping it together. "Oh, Lord, maybe I can find something to do in the kitchen."

"You mean, before he sees you?"

Pru managed a weak grin. "My yellow stripe is showing, huh?"

Indeed she was keeping herself tucked in the corner of the booth, her back to Chance, where he couldn't possibly see her. And the kitchen door was merely a short dash from where she sat. She felt that yellow stripe grow wider.

"I've never known you to run from a problem before, Pru."

"I've never been in this position before...." She took a big breath. "So what's he doing?"

Looking for her?

"Reba's seating him...oh...about two booths behind you."

"In *my* section?"

"Looks like fate, doesn't it?"

"More like bad luck."

Alcina was grinning at her. So nice that *she* was amused! Just wait until Reed came back to Silver Springs and it was *her* turn to sweat. Pru downed the rest of her tea, but rather than feel calm, she felt even more jittery than before.

A moment later Reba paused at their booth, saying, "Customer, honey, break's over," then whisked into the kitchen herself.

*Right.*

Gritting her teeth, Pru slipped out of the booth and exchanged an agonized look with Alcina, whose expression immediately grew concerned.

"Chance keeps coming back for *something,* Pru," she said softly. "If it helps any, my guess would be that something is *you.*"

Not knowing what to believe when it came to Chance, Pru pulled herself together and approached his booth. His hat was off and as he gave the menu his attention, his hair gleamed with ribbons of dark gold.

A trick of the overhead light, Pru thought, trying not to be affected. Even so, her fingers itched to tangle in his hair—maybe this time to give it a good pull!

She found her breath and cleared her throat. "Can I take your drink order?"

Chance's head jerked up, and from his expression she got the idea that he was truly surprised to see her.

"What are you doing here?"

Feigning nonchalance, she indicated the Reba's Café apron tied around her waist. "My name is Pru and I'll be your server this evening."

"But what are you *doing* here?"

"Uh, working. Or trying to."

"This is a little removed from nursing, isn't it?" Chance asked. Suddenly his mobile mouth split into a grin. "Or did you off a patient who aggravated—"

"How about a beer to quench your thirst?" Pru cut in. She didn't owe him any explanations.

Obviously determined to get one, Chance asked, "Or are you just filling in for a friend?"

"We have Bud, Mich and Miller on tap." Pru was determined to stay cool, to pretend he was just another customer. "In bottles we—"

"I'll have a Corona."

She raised an eyebrow. *His* tastes certainly had changed. "With or without lime?"

He was halfway through answering, "Definitely with," when she spun away from him to the small bar. There she put in her order and took a series of deep breaths.

No respite for the wicked, though. One of her customers was waving her over for the bill. She quickly took care of that table, swooped the beer off the bar and set it in front of a seemingly disbelieving Chance. He was staring as if he'd never before seen her.

"Have you decided?" she asked, pencil poised to her order pad.

"Decided?"

"What you want."

His gaze was glued to her pad—no, to her hand. Was he checking for a ring? "I knew what I wanted long ago, Miss Prudence."

She rolled her eyes to cover the discomfort she felt at the nickname that conjured intimate memories. "Your food. I assume you're here to eat."

To her horror, Pru realized that he was staring at the thin silver bracelet decorating her wrist. Of course he must recognize it. Double damnation! The restaurant always got so warm that she'd favored a short-sleeved lime-green shirt rather than one with longer sleeves that might have hidden the token of affection Chance had bought her years ago.

"Is that the way you always speak to customers?"

Angry at herself that she hadn't tossed away the bracelet the way he'd done her heart, Pru quipped, "Only the ones who ask for it."

Gaze fixed behind her, Chance waved. "Maybe Reba would be interested—"

"Chance, no, please!" she hissed, immediately dropping the studied attitude. "I can't lose this job."

But Reba had already arrived. "Do we have a problem here?" she asked, looking from one to the other.

"Indeed, we do," Chance drawled, then gave her one of his infamous grins. "Miss Prudence here was mighty stumped. She couldn't decide which to recommend more highly—the grilled pork chops or the Pueblo platter."

"Oh, well...I guess that depends on whether you're in the mood for savory or spicy."

"Spicy." His blue eyes fairly glowed as he winked at Pru. "The spicier the better."

"Then you'll want to go for the Pueblo Platter," Reba said, expression turning suspicious. "The chile *relleños* are smoking tonight."

"That'll do...for starters." He didn't take his gaze from Pru's. "Thanks for the help, Reba."

As if finally catching on that Chance was flirting with the help, Reba gave him an amused look. "No problem, hon. You just treat my server here good."

"My intention exactly."

"And don't take up all of her time. She has other customers."

"Loud and clear, Reba."

Pru silently counted to five as the still-amused woman moved to check on customers at another table. She felt as if her boss and her former lover were sharing some kind of an inside joke and she was the outsider.

No sooner did Pru open her mouth to give him what-for than Chance put up a warning hand.

"Careful," he murmured through a continuing, too-charming grin. "The boss's got an eye out in this direction."

"Just one?"

"It wouldn't be hard to get her full attention again."

It took willpower not to smack him.

"Look, Chance, I thought I was clear about not wanting to see you."

"I'm here. I'm hungry. I'm not going anywhere."

She couldn't help herself. "I find *that* impossible to believe."

Chance's smile faded. "Like I said, we should go somewhere private to talk."

His tone was serious. Almost urgent. Pru had to fight herself to keep her resolve.

"You can talk right now. You have a couple of choices with the Pueblo Platter—starting with whether you want the chicken or shredded beef tamale."

Chance seemed to get the message—at least temporarily. He gave up and got down to the business of ordering. And Pru made certain he received exactly what he'd said he wanted—*the spicier the better!*

As she moved around her station, taking care of other customers, she surreptitiously kept an eye on Chance. It did her heart good to watch his face redden as he ate every jalapeño-laden bite of food.

Gradually, on her way back from the kitchen with an order, she became aware of something else.

Rather, *someone.*

A shadowy figure stood outside, to the right of the plate-glass window. At first she thought this was a customer waiting for a supper companion or maybe one taking a last drag on his cigarette before entering. Unlike other New Mexican establishments, Reba's Café had a no smoking policy.

As she passed the window on her way back to the kitchen, a now-curious Pru tried to get a better look…but as she gazed into the dark, the figure faded straight back into the shadows, the furtive movement reminding her of the creepy sensation she'd had when she'd thought she was being followed earlier.

Then she shook off the odd feeling and went on with her business.

She didn't spot the figure again.

A few minutes later she realized that Alcina was gathering her things, getting ready to leave. Noting that a red-faced Chance was scraping his plate clean, Pru purposely drifted by her friend's booth.

"So how did it go?" Alcina asked.

Pru crowed, "Let's say I got some satisfaction out of being his server."

The other woman's pale eyebrows rose. "Uh-oh. You didn't inflict permanent damage, I hope?"

"Fortunately for him, no."

Sliding out of her booth, Alcina rose and gave Pru a conspiratorial smile and a quick, one-armed hug. "Keep me apprised of the battle's progress, would you?"

"I'll call you to note any major victories," Pru promised with a grin.

But when it came time for Chance to settle the bill, her spirits sank.

Handing him the modest accounting, she was torn between wanting to help him out the door and wanting to lock it so he couldn't go anywhere. But that was her heart arguing with itself. It had nothing to do with her head.

So she said, "Chance, please don't do this again."

"What? Eat here?" He pulled a twenty from his wallet. "I don't think Reba would appreciate—"

"I don't appreciate your keeping after me when I've told you how I feel."

"You've only told me part of it," Chance contended. "The part you want me to know."

"You're wrong," she muttered, taking his money.

"Am I?"

"You always did have an inflated sense of self-worth."

The callous words were out of her mouth before she could stop them. Thing was, she knew they weren't true. That, if anything, he preened and joked to cover his insecurity. Self-worth was an elusive thing unless nurtured by family. And Chance's family had done anything but nurture him in any way, as far as she could see.

Now *she'd* hurt him. She saw it in the way the light in his eyes dimmed and his smile grew stiff. She sensed a wave of desolation that made her stomach knot and her chest squeeze tight.

He deserved it, she told herself. He deserved the same thing he'd done to her. More.

But Pru wasn't a cruel person. Guilt washed through her as she tried to hand Chance his change.

"Keep it," he said stiffly.

"No." She set it on the table in front of him. "I don't want anything from you, Chance. Nothing at all."

None of the things he was willing to give…not without the rest.

Expression closed, Chance rose and walked away without another word.

Pru stared down at the money, far too large for a tip. She hesitated only a moment before her practical side took over. Then she scooped up the bills and coins and stuffed them in her pocket.

Not for her but for Hope—she'd think of it as child support and fight the growing guilt that Chance didn't even know that he had a child.

That was *his* doing, not hers!

Unable to help herself, Pru watched Chance exit the restaurant without ever looking back.

She was just turning to another customer when a flash of movement caught her attention—slipping from the shadows to the right of the big plate glass window, a dark figure traveled in the same direction.

Was she imagining things or was Chance being followed?

## Chapter Four

Leaving Reba's Café, Chance decided that he wasn't ready to return to the Curly-Q—which would mean facing his brother and old man, something he'd like to avoid a while longer—and that he was done tooling around on his motorcycle for a while. He also could use a drink.

The Silver Slipper Saloon was the only bar in town, so he headed straight for it.

Two years hadn't changed the place. The long room of dark wood held a massive bar, and behind it, an oversize Mexican silver-framed mirror. At one end of the room there was a raised stage area with electric footlights. Most of the bulbs were still missing, he noted. And the bar's walls were still hung with aging posters of acts that had appeared there more than a decade ago.

Mostly men populated the place, at small tables. Only one guy was at the bar, and he at the other end.

Chance slid onto a stool and got the immediate attention of the bartender. *He* was new, at least since Chance was last in Silver Springs, though Chance got the feeling he'd seen the guy before, somewhere. Fortyish, the man was large and had rough features topped by a silver-blond buzz-cut too distinctive to forget.

The bartender's pale gray, nearly colorless eyes narrowed on Chance. "What can I do for you?"

"A beer with lime."

The man nodded and reached into the cooler. "Hugh Ruskin." He introduced himself as he topped the bottle with a wedge of lime and set it down on the bar, gold and diamond ring too fancy for a bartender weighing down his hand. "And you must be one of the Quarrels boys."

Surprised, Chance grinned. "Chance Quarrels. So what is it that gives me away? The family resemblance?" Of which there was none—he didn't look like either of his brothers or the old man. Felice had always told him he was the spitting image of his mother, Sunny. "Or the Curly-Q brand on my forehead?"

"We don't get many strangers." Even as Ruskin said it, one walked through the bar door.

Another stranger to Chance, anyway. He watched the dark-haired man with a handlebar mustache seat himself at the bar several stools away. The guy never so much as glanced in Chance's direction.

"News goes through this town as fast as a speeding bullet," Ruskin was saying. "I already heard son number two arrived before I got to the bar."

"Make that number three." Chance clarified, "I'm low man on the totem pole."

Ruskin grinned, showing lots of teeth. "I don't care where you are in the lineup as long as you stay thirsty."

Snorting to himself, the bartender moved off to

take care of the new arrival, leaving Chance to his own devices.

His thoughts strayed to Pru as they inevitably did.

Her sweet, innocent scent lingered in his mind—like dewy flower petals on a spring morning. At times that scent was soothing, at times soul shattering.

In his mind's eye, he could see Pru's full, tempting, woman's hips and bottom hugged by tight jeans. His fingers ached to release her curly hair from that ponytail, to stroke the loose strands kissing her lightly freckled face. He could almost feel her competent yet gentle hands on every inch of his body.

Her hands...

He hadn't missed that hand-worked silver and sugalite bracelet that Pru had been wearing. He'd bought it for her after his first major saddle-bronc win several years back. He couldn't help but wonder about the significance of her wearing it tonight.

Surely if she were done with him, she would have buried the thing long ago.

That bracelet had double significance, Chance remembered. The win that had given him the extra cash to buy it had been a turning point for him. A reason to quit day work and turn his serious attention to rodeoing. That's when he'd decided to go for it, to make his mark in the rodeo world, to get enough monetary return so that he could have the option to do something meaningful with the rest of his life.

Something that would be *his*.

Off and on, he'd thought about getting a spread of his own, but that didn't hold a lot of appeal for him. That was his father's world—and Reed's—not his. He'd always preferred horses to cows. He wouldn't discount the possibility of ranching altogether, but he had another, more interesting idea brewing at the back of his mind.

A rodeo school.

Problem was he was no Ty Murray. He didn't have a big name known throughout the international rodeo world. But he was chipping away at it, Chance thought. If he stuck with it for a couple more years...

Oddly enough, he was getting more and more weary of the circuit that, for a while, had been his life's blood. All the picking up and going two or three times a week was getting to him. He hadn't realized how badly until lately, wasn't sure if he really was ready to give up the road, but the notion was there to be brought out and examined from all angles.

Chance just knew he was tired and longed for something different than he'd experienced so far in his thirty years. Something that would satisfy him and let him see a certain red-haired woman as often as he pleased.

Something that would win the approval of Prudence Prescott, preacher's daughter.

Sounded like he was ready to commit himself. Damn!

He broke out into a cold sweat even thinking about it.

Again, the door swung open behind him.

"Well, I'll be...if it ain't Chance Quarrels himself."

Recognizing the voice, Chance slid around on his stool. "Will Spencer! I heard you were dogging me."

Will held out a gloved hand, and Chance grasped

it in a firm shake. Probably a few years older than he, Will was still pretty enough, with his deep tan, curly golden-blond hair and light golden-brown eyes, to get the buckle bunnies fighting each other for his attention.

"Actually, I was just passing through Silver Springs and thinking about seeing if you were around, when I ran into your brother Bart," Will said. "He made me an offer I couldn't refuse."

"Cowboy pay for Billy-Boy Spencer?"

"Sometimes that looks like a fortune—all depends on a man's point of view."

"You got hurt that bad on the Fourth?"

Will had drawn a particularly nasty bull, Chance remembered. One who'd gored him when he was down. He'd been taken from the arena on a wooden stretcher, and his recovery hadn't been swift.

Chance hated bull riding, though to be really successful—to win the all-around titles—he would have to get over that. Another reason he wanted to quit.

"I could go back." Will slid onto the stool next to Chance. "Nothing's stopping me physically—I healed up okay. I guess I just don't have the heart for rodeoing any more."

Considering he'd been having like thoughts, Chance said, "We must be getting old."

"Yeah, and I kinda lost the incentive. She wasn't the kind of woman who stuck around when a man was down."

So he'd lost his woman in addition to his competitive spirit, Chance thought. He could empathize. "A real shame."

"Yeah, but I think I found me a way to win her back."

Chance raised his drink in salute. "Whatever it takes."

Then the bartender approached them. "Hey, Will, the usual?"

Will gave Ruskin a thumb's-up, then turned back to Chance. "Yeah, the work's hard," he admitted, "and the pay's lousy, but it's a life a lot of guys choose, I guess. And if it's good enough for you..."

"You don't have a rainy-day fund to get you started in something else?" Chance asked.

Will had done almost as well as he had—even better with the bulls until that terrible accident.

"No insurance. The medical bills and just surviving while I recuperated ate up the little I had." Will shrugged fatalistically. "Besides, I don't mind day work, and you and me on the range together will be like old times."

Not that they'd ever worked together before—not exactly. They'd been friendly competitors, going from state to state to the same rodeos, but they'd never ridden the circuit as a team the way some cowboys did.

"Yeah, we'll be working together for the moment," Chance said.

"What moment? You're not already thinking about picking up stakes and moving on?" Will seemed surprised. "You just got here."

"But I'm not sure how long I'll be staying."

"Rodeo's in your blood, huh?"

"It's not that." Reluctant to bring up the one subject that might put him at odds with Will, he chose to be evasive. "There's something I have to do, is all."

"Sounds serious."

"It *is* serious. I don't have a choice."

"A man's always got choices," Will said. "He's gotta look out for himself."

"Not always," Chance said grimly, remembering that photo of Alvarez and the family that had been left behind. He couldn't live with himself if he pretended that hadn't happened. "Not this time."

"Whatever you say, partner, whatever you say."

Ruskin set a draft in front of Will and got talky once more. "Heard you boys had some bad luck over on the Curly-Q this afternoon."

His expression dark, Will said, "Yeah, Frank Ewing almost got his arm chewed up by a post-hole digger. You wouldn't have heard any rumors about who might have downed some of the Curly-Q's fences?"

Ruskin raised his hands and backed off. "Hey, I keep my nose out of other people's business."

Thinking the bartender had been pretty nosy and somewhat knowledgeable earlier, Chance added, "Yeah, but drunken cowboys like to talk, and they usually have the ear of their favorite bartender."

"They don't do that kind of talking to this one," Ruskin said. "I haven't been around long enough for the locals to trust me."

So he *was* new in town. Before Chance could quiz him on his background, Ruskin got busy, taking himself from behind the bar to one of the small tables where three men who looked vaguely familiar sat.

Wondering how much Will knew, Chance took a sip of his beer and said, "I hear the Curly-Q's been having lots of bad luck lately."

"Yeah, some. Maybe more that I don't know

about—I've only been around about as long as our friend there.'' He indicated the bartender.

"This bad luck—could the incidents be connected?''

"Hard to say.'' Will's brow furrowed. "Cows getting sick…windmills breaking down…cowboys dying…they don't exactly make some kind of pattern, do they?''

*Cowboys dying?*

"You must not have heard,'' Chance said. "Frank Ewing's going to be all right.''

"Yeah, I know, and I'm glad. He's an upstanding kinda guy.''

"Then what are you talking about?'' Chance asked. "What cowboys died?''

"Only one, actually,'' Will clarified. "A green kid named Peter Dagget rode a horse he was told to stay away from. Horse dumped him but his foot got caught in a stirrup. His neck was broken.''

A terrible tragedy…

"But it was an accident, right?'' Chance asked.

"Sure looked like it, though Josie isn't 100 percent. Thought maybe the kid got in the way when her ex was after her. Oh, that's Josie Walker, by the way—Curly-Q's wrangler.''

"Haven't met the lady yet.''

Will proceeded to tell him about how she'd started out taking care of the ranch horses and had quickly become the woman in Chance's brother's life. A victim of a car accident while trying to get away from the ex-husband who'd been after her, Josie had landed at the Curly-Q as wrangler. Will also said that she hadn't been able to remember her real name or much else at first because of a head injury in that accident.

"Her ex-husband might have succeeded in killing her if not for Bart's help," Will told him.

"That's Saint Bart," Chance said. "Once a law-man, always a lawman."

"Her memory is back now," Will assured him. "Maybe you know her from the circuit—she's a bar-rel racer. Already qualified for the Nationals."

Which meant she was one of the best.

"Name's familiar," Chance admitted, figuring Jo-sie must have been the woman in the kitchen with Felice. He was better with faces than with names, though. "I've probably seen her race, but I don't know her."

"If you saw her take that flaxen-maned sorrel of hers around a couple of barrels, you'd never forget it." Will's expression grew serious once more. "So how long will Frank be out?"

"At least a couple of days, I heard."

"We're short-handed as is—lucky you showed up at the right time."

Not that he was going to be around long enough to make a difference, Chance thought, suddenly hav-ing one more thing to feel guilty about. It sounded like the Curly-Q needed all the help it could get.

"It probably wouldn't hurt to put the word out that we're looking for more help," he said.

"Think your brother will agree to hire someone else?"

The question raised Chance's hackles. "Bart isn't the only word on the subject." They were supposed to have equal say in the ranch, after all. "It *is* a family corporation."

Will called out, "Hey, Ruskin, know anyone looking for day work?"

Standing at a table of four, the bartender said with a snort, "Nah, these guys are too lazy to work—they all got women to support them."

Which caused a flurry of protests but no volunteers from the table.

A gravelly voice from their left said, "I'm available. Kleef Hatsfield."

Chance looked past Will to the guy with the handlebar mustache. His dark eyes, kind of beady and narrow set, were steady on him.

"Experience?" Chance asked.

"My mama claimed a horse gave birth to me on the range."

"How much do you like hard work?"

"No more than the next man. But I do whatever it takes to keep a roof over my head, food in my stomach and me in folding money."

"What's your specialty?"

"I'm as good at one thing as another."

Chance kept the questions coming, but Kleef continued to be evasive. Normally he could read a man as easily as a deck of cards, but this one was an exception. There was something off about him—he just couldn't put his finger on it. Still, they did need more help at the ranch. Giving the guy a try couldn't hurt anything.

So, after talking to Kleef a while longer, Chance told him to show up at the bunkhouse first thing in the morning.

The man immediately got up from the bar. "If I'm gonna be up at dawn, I'd better get some shut-eye." He tossed back the rest of his drink and then left.

Will looked down into his own beer. "That was sure a surprise, partner."

"What?"

"Your taking such an interest in the Curly-Q. Hiring a hand…you're acting like a boss rather than a man planning to skedaddle."

"I don't want to see the ranch fail just because I'm not going to be around."

Will chewed on that for a minute before saying, "So you really *are* leaving."

"I told you I had something important to do."

"Yeah, you sure did. Well, I'll be sorry to see you go." Will slid off his stool and lowered the brim of his hat over his eyes. "I guess I'd better be getting back to the bunkhouse myself."

Chance knew he should do the same, but he said, "Catch you later," and drew on the beer.

He was surprised at himself, too—*him hiring a day worker!* He'd break the news to Bart and Pa as soon as he got back to the spread. Though why he looked forward to it with such relish, he couldn't say. After all, he wasn't going to be around long, and that would lose him his stake in the place.

He ought to leave the details to Saint Bart, Chance thought sourly.

When his beer bottle was empty, he looked around to say good-night to Ruskin, but the bartender was off in the back. So he wandered out into the mild November night. Instead of heading directly for his motorcycle, however, he crossed the street and stopped in the shadows of Reba's Café. The place was nearly empty. Pru stood back at the servers' station, alone, appearing lost in thought.

Was she thinking about him? Chance wondered.

Was he on her mind every bit as often as she was on his?

He considered waiting for her until the café closed. But he would be pressing her, the very thing she'd asked him to stop doing.

Patience, he told himself. Patience and a charming smile would get him farther than any aggressive action.

Regretfully, shoulders slumped, he turned away from the window. How much patience would she need? he wondered. Probably more than circumstance allowed.

Having arrived in town at the height of the supper hour, he'd had to park his motorcycle on a nearby side street.

Despite the dark, he found his way around as easily as if he'd never left town. Ironic that the place he couldn't think of as home was so imprinted on his memory.

As was the woman he kept returning to see.

Chance was so preoccupied with thoughts of Pru that the shuffling sounds behind him barely registered.

In his head, he was seeing her…smelling her…touching her…

As he neared the motorcycle, he dug into his pocket and pulled out the key chain. His fingers levered the ignition key until something hard smacked into the back of his elbow and triggered a chain reaction—his arm automatically shot forward, the keys flying from his hand.

"What the hell!" he growled.

Spinning to see what had hit him, Chance was

blindsided. Pain streaked his right cheek and a flash lit his mind.

He teetered then and blindly threw himself forward onto his attacker. They danced for a moment, Chance's arms locked around a muscular chest. The man was of a height with him, but even if there had been streetlights, he wouldn't have been able to see the face. He could vaguely make out a brimmed hat shoved down to the eyes and a bandanna from the nose down.

A scuffle from behind warned him seconds too late. Even so, Chance wasn't prepared for the shock that sizzled through his back. He spasmed and staggered free of his attacker, then, unable to duck, saw the fist that came flying at him.

Hot pain seared his lower lip as the flesh sliced open against his teeth. The warm salty taste of his own blood filled his mouth, threatening to choke him.

Chance didn't have to ask why. He knew. But, spitting blood, he put it to words, anyway. "What do you want from me?"

His answer came in the form of more pain—this time crashing down against his skull. He flew face forward, put his arms out to regain his balance. But he kept going down...down...down to the dirt road.

Then a set of hands attacked him, rifling through his clothing. He heard the sound of crinkling paper as he reached out to stop them and stumbled to his feet, again doing a strange dance with one of his attackers.

A jolt ran up his arm, stunning him a second time, making his heart trip out of rhythm. He went weak in the knees. Found himself falling. Landed hard on his side.

Before he could recover, a boot toe crashed into his solar plexus.

He couldn't breathe....

As he gasped for air, his head going light and the world around him dimming, he heard one of them growl, "Get out, Quarrels, before it's too late!"

PRU LEFT REBA'S, thoughts of Chance Quarrels dancing through her head.

After he'd left, she'd relived private moments they'd spent together: the first time they'd kissed; the first time he'd tried taking it further and she'd turned him away; the first time they'd made love.

She tried to erase those memories, really she did, but nothing worked. He was there in her mind...

Teasing her...

Taunting her...

Tempting her.

And so, every fiber of her being was alive as Pru pierced the dark with her expectant gaze, searching for the one man who made her feel like a real woman. The *only* man who ever had. Some instinct had warned her that he'd been around after he'd left earlier—it had been as if his gaze was on her—but apparently, this time her instincts led her astray.

She was almost disappointed.

Well, okay, she *was* disappointed, she admitted. Part of her. The part of her that had no sense!

She'd parked on a side street. No lights, but a moon that slid behind a bank of clouds. She could just make out the shape of her old station wagon when a moan nearby startled her and made her jump.

''Who's there?'' she asked.

She hooked the car keys between her fingers, points out, a makeshift weapon.

Again a moan. More protracted this time. Sounding like someone in agony.

The hair at the back of her neck stood up.

She pinned the location of the sound and was torn between finding out what was going on and getting into her vehicle and driving off. She could call for professional help when she was safe.

A scuffling and more moans—low, on the road— made her pulse zing.

''Who's there?'' she asked again, all senses alert, this time sidling toward her vehicle.

But once inside, she couldn't put her keys in the ignition. Couldn't leave behind someone in trouble, someone who sounded hurt, not even if she meant to call for help. She was, after all, a nurse at heart, even if she was waiting tables for a living.

She fished under her seat for her flashlight. A snag in the metal bit her hand, and she let out a sharp shriek. Double damnation, she was jumpy! Grabbing the flashlight, she opened the driver's door, slid out of the station wagon and hurriedly retraced her steps.

''Hey, uh, I'm going to help you,'' she called out. ''Okay?''

Another moan, slurred words. ''Pru, 's me...''

The hair on her arms rose. She clicked on the flashlight and found him in its beam. He was trying to get himself into an upright position. His long hair was loose and tossed around his face. His cheek was bruised, and blood dripped from his mouth.

''Oh, Lord!'' she said with a gasp, fighting the nausea of fear. ''Chance!''

## Chapter Five

Heart in her throat, Pru flew the short distance to him and dropped to her knees. Hardly able to breathe, she choked out, "Chance, what happened?"

"Got mugged…" he ground out, then followed the claim with a loopy grin that appeared grotesque amidst the blood. "…dizzy."

*A head injury!*

She was trying not to panic. "I need to check your eyes." Her own stung with the threat of tears. "Keep them open."

"'kay."

All professional now, she shone the beam of the flashlight and stared into them for a moment, long enough to determine that he didn't have a concussion. She had him follow her fingers and tell her how many she had raised. Then she took his wrist and found his pulse—a little thready but not alarmingly so.

Reassured, she felt her own pulse slowing. "Where does it hurt?"

"Everywhere…"

His voice was hoarse and thick as though he were having trouble getting out even that one word.

"Anything broken?"

"Hope not." He moved around a bit, testing limbs. A grunt of pain escaped him. "Damn shoulder…"

"Again?" Not a new injury, Pru knew, but at least it wasn't serious.

A quick visual inspection revealed a few contusions on his face in addition to the blood, mostly dried, but a bit still dribbling from his lower lip where it had split open. A fierce anger filled her, and Pru wanted to roast whoever did this over an open barbecue pit.

"Do you think you can stand, if I help you?" she asked.

He was already raising himself. "I'll try…"

Pru hooked an arm around his waist. "Let me know if I'm hurting you in any way."

Chance placed his left arm across her back, and he cradled his right close to his body, protecting his shoulder.

Though Pru tried to ignore the sensation of his body pressed to hers, she was fighting a losing battle. The flesh *was* weak. At least hers was when it got too close to his.

This was professional not personal, she reminded herself, trying to trick her body into cooperating with her mind.

*Yeah, right!*

Somehow she helped Chance to his feet. Starting to let him go, she felt him teeter and renewed her grip around his waist. His weight pressed against her as she drew him toward her station wagon. They were now hip to hip, waist to waist, side to side. The close contact reminded her of how warm he got—a human electric blanket at night.

She nearly choked with the memory. "Hang in there for just a little while longer," she said. "I'll get you to a hospital as fast as I can."

"No hospital."

She tried to reason with him. "But you could be seriously injured."

"No hospital!"

"Doc Baxter, then."

"No. You."

"I'm not qualified—"

"*You,*" he stubbornly repeated, stopping dead in his tracks a few yards from the vehicle. "I want you."

She wasn't fool enough to think he only meant medically. He was using this as a way to get to her.

If she insisted on letting someone else take care of him, Chance might refuse to come with her at all, Pru knew. He could be pigheaded when it came to his own safety or personal well-being. She could see it now—him marching back to his motorcycle, and, idiot that he could be, trying to ride it home.

Reviewing her options—none that she could think of—she caved.

"All right. I'll make a deal with you, Chance. I'll take you home and patch you up as best I can. But if I think there's anything serious going on—*anything*—you'll let me take you to the hospital."

"Deal."

Too easy. Suspicious she might be, but she would have to take him at his word or worry about him all night.

Chance seemed a bit steadier on his feet those last

few yards to the station wagon. He leaned less heavily on her, yet he remained too close for comfort. Pru was relieved to get him in the passenger seat and her behind the wheel. She drove off carefully, trying to avoid any big bumps lest she hurt him even more.

When she pulled herself together, she asked, "How's your head feeling?"

"Clearing."

"And your shoulder?"

"How do you think?"

That shoulder of his had been a problem for years, starting with a bad throw off a bull, Pru knew. Even a bronc ride could mess it up. But normally he was able to manipulate it back in line himself.

They drove in silence, Pru stewing about the fix she was in, bringing him into the danger zone—which would be anywhere Hope was—Chance suffering without complaint.

The house was already dark. Mitch and Justine usually retired early, not too long after getting their little girls down for the night. When she waitressed, they took care of Hope, as well. Pru suspected they also took advantage of those nights to have a little personal time alone.

Quietly she helped Chance inside, through the kitchen and into her bedroom, all the while aware that their daughter slept a mere room away. She was taking too great a gamble here, Pru feared, but what else could she do?

"Take your shirt off and get on the bed," she told Chance, letting go of his waist.

"Yes, ma'am!" he said with more energy than

she'd heard since finding him. "I thought you'd never ask."

"And don't get any ideas! This is professional, not personal."

If she repeated that enough, maybe she'd believe it herself. One of the nightstands held a small lamp with a mica shade. She turned it on. It cast a soft golden glow over his bare chest—he was in the process of removing his shirt—and her mouth went dry.

Escape into the bathroom next door was a relief. There she gathered a basin of warm water, a washcloth and a big first aid kit—at present her single link to the profession she'd hoped to pursue. Getting pregnant had thrown a wrench into her plans, and she still had those last couple of courses to take.

Maybe someday…

In the bedroom a shirtless Chance was sitting on her bed, still nursing his shoulder. She would get to that injury eventually, after she cleaned him up and checked him out more thoroughly. Avoiding looking at the expanse of golden chest marred by darkening bruises, she wrung warm water from the washcloth.

"Let's clean you up and see if you shine beneath all that war paint," she joked.

Humor helped her keep her perspective, especially when she had to step in closer to Chance to get to his face. She found herself wedged nicely between his knees. Careful not to get dangerously closer, she gently tilted his chin and raised it so she could better see what she was doing. The long strands of his hair framing his face slid back, away from the features that had been brutalized.

A wave of sickness passed through her, that anyone could so viciously mar his beautiful face.

As she cautiously dabbed away the blood from his chin and mouth, Chance murmured, ''Be gentle with me, Miss Prudence.'' He widened his blue eyes, locking them onto hers.

A frisson of sensation washed through her at the very sound of his low, suddenly vibrant voice.

''Don't get any ideas!'' Considering she was getting enough for them both, she needed to find a way to distract herself, so again, she asked, ''What happened?''

''I told you—''

''Details.''

''Two guys mugged me. They were wearing hats and bandannas over their faces.''

''As soon as I'm done checking you over, I'll call the sheriff's office.''

''No.''

''You got robbed, and you're not going to report it?''

''I wasn't robbed. I was mugged.''

''Well, that alone—''

''No.''

*No* seemed to be his favorite word of the night.

Once more she tried to reason with him. ''So what? You expect Bart to handle this with everything else he has on his back?''

The good humor dissipated from his voice when he said, ''Saint Bart doesn't need to know.''

Fear reared its ugly head. ''Chance, what's going on?'' she asked, unable to hide her alarm. ''Please, the truth.'' What kind of trouble was he in?

''Nothing you need to worry about.''

But she was worried, not about his physical condition—he was bruised and battered, but as far as she could tell, not seriously hurt—but about why two men would want to mug him and why he wouldn't want to do anything about it.

Tight-lipped, she continued her inspection of his face. She smoothed back the long strands of hair that had slipped free of the leather tie, trying to keep her touch impersonal when she really wanted to tangle her fingers in its thickness.

A wicked bruise brushed his cheek with color. But his lip—his wonderfully sensual lower lip—was swollen and split. It probably could use a stitch or two, but she didn't expect he'd listen to her about it. She put out a hand as if her touch could heal it...then changed her mind.

But before she could withdraw her hand, he caught her wrist and kissed her fingers.

She flushed straight down to her toes.

"Chance, please..."

"I always aim to please."

Still holding her wrist, he turned her hand and kissed the inside of her palm. His lips were soothing, his tongue seductive, his teeth electrifying. When he gently bit into the fleshy base of her thumb, Pru felt her knees go weak, and she swayed forward.

Chance snaked an arm around her and pulled her closer. The heat of him held her transfixed. His hand cupped her bottom and slid to more intimate places. Her thighs spread for him as if with a will of their own.

"Chance..." she whispered, realizing she was losing control.

"Yes, Miss Prudence?"

Her name had never sounded so sexy, she thought hazily as his mouth found the tip of her breast. He nuzzled her nipple through her shirt and bra and, as it extended, tugged at the hard point of flesh.

Her body lit like a Fourth of July display.

Her flesh *was* weak, most definitely.

She locked her fingers in his hair and threw back her head, only vaguely aware of the lump her fingers touched. He undid two buttons and nudged the material to the side. His lips on her breast made her squirm closer and push at him with her hips. One of her knees was wedged in his groin, and she felt him grow hard and long against it. Then all she could think about was how good he would feel inside her, against her already-swollen flesh.

Before she could stop him, Chance was opening the waistband of her jeans, tugging at the zipper, slipping in where no other man had ever touched her. His fingers easily slid inside her aroused folds. She was wet and slippery and more filled with desire than she ever had been before.

Chance obviously knew it, too....

Trailing his lips from her breast to her neck, he lay back, levering her whole body over his. One hand cradled the back of her neck as he pulled her face toward him.

His tongue slid into her mouth...slowly...fully...ravishingly...making her aware of another area that needed like attention. Then the sharp metallic taste of his blood reminded her that he was hurt.

Even so, she couldn't resist one mind-plummeting, soul-shattering kiss. The kind of kiss she had dreamed about every night of every week of every month since she last saw him.

*If only...if only...*

The kiss went on and on, reminding her of how much she loved him. How much she missed him. Tempting her with giving in, letting herself succumb to his mouth and hands that knew her so well.

She was rocking against his fingers as she rose higher, pushed harder. Her mind hazed over, even as she tried to convince herself to stop.

The problem was she didn't really want to stop.

Then his thumb caught her most sensitive spot, created a live-wire friction that held her, mindless and panting, wanting more.

"C'mon, Miss Prudence," he coaxed in a whisper. "Let go. Let go for me. C'mon…"

"Wait…Chance, wait…"

Her words died off as he bit her earlobe, then laved the shell with the tip of his tongue. His fingers stilled where they were, yet sensation roiled in every fiber of her being, threatening to rip her apart.

"I don't want you to wait," he murmured. He flicked his thumbnail against her teasingly. "I want to feel you shudder inside."

He nipped at her neck, ran little kisses along its length from jaw to shoulder.

"I want to hear those sounds you make when you can't hold on any longer," he insisted. "Greedy, pouty sounds." He trailed his tongue around to her sweet spot. "Tell me you want it," he murmured. "Unless you want me to stop right now, tell me!"

Pru was lost. "Yes, oh, yes!" she breathed, sliding fingers into his hair, pulling it free from the leather tie.

She anchored herself with his hair as Chance increased the friction of his thumb and deepened the thrust of his fingers. All the while he talked to her, murmuring encouragement against her throat, along her cheek.

"Love me, Pru, c'mon. Let me feel how much."

All too quickly her body gave what her mind had at first tried to deny him. Sounds over which she had no control issued from deep in her throat.

"That's it," he whispered. "Let go. For me, Pru. Let go for me."

For a moment she froze, drifted on a high, until wave upon wave of pleasure pulsed through her and around those fingers that never stopped moving against her and in her until she grabbed his wrist, murmuring, "Please, no more."

The Fourth of July fireworks had never been this good, she thought, a sob catching in her throat as her muscles gave way and she melted against him.

"Ah, Miss Prudence, I knew you could be spectacular."

Chance wrapped both arms around her and held her tight.

Both arms!

*His shoulder...*

Through a haze of fulfillment, Pru realized his shoulder seemed to be just fine now...if it had even been pulled in the first place.

The suspicion led to a spurt of anger.

How dare he seduce her, when she'd made it perfectly clear that she wasn't interested?

How dare she let him? another voice whispered. Some will she had!

She could have stopped him at any time—Pru knew that. He never would have forced her. But in the end, as always, Chance Quarrels had proved to be irresistible.

Hugely embarrassed at her own weakness, at the fact that he had taken her over the edge, that he had enjoyed watching without joining her, she pushed at his chest.

"Chance, let go of me."

"Aw, Prunella, don't be that way."

But he let go…and she somehow, miraculously, stumbled back off him and onto her feet.

Still on his back, his knees sprawled open, Chance rose to his elbows. Pru's pulse trip-hammered as she took him in visually, so seductive looking despite his bruises that he made her knees shake. She might have found nirvana, but he was still fully aroused—those tight jeans of his couldn't hide it.

Which only made her feel worse.

Staring down at the floor, she choked out, "I'll go get you an ice pack."

He lifted an eyebrow at her. "I don't think that'll cure what ails me."

"For your face!"

He wore a self-satisfied grin that made her want to smack him. No, then he would groan and moan about how she'd made him hurt worse and she would probably feel such guilt that she would just have to nurse him again.

Pru backed out of the room, wondering again who had attacked him and why…not to mention how she'd let him get to her after all her fancy promises to herself.

CHANCE'S GRIN FALTERED the moment Pru turned her back on him and whipped through the doorway. With a groan he lay back on the bed and adjusted himself, as if that would make him more comfortable. His pulse was thready, his breath came hard, and he had an itch he couldn't scratch, but he didn't give a damn about that.

He wanted Pru, but more important, he wanted her to want him.

And she had.

For the moment, anyway.

Chance savored the small victory.

For a short while, he'd been able to hold her, to touch her, to do things to her that he'd only dreamt of for the last two years. But he'd wanted it to be about Pru and her needs. He wanted to give her that from his heart. His own needs could wait a while longer. He didn't mind waiting until she was really ready to give him her all.

When she was ready, making love would happen naturally between them—he wouldn't have to put on the charm or make a special effort to seduce her.

Not that he'd planned it this time.

But when opportunity had knocked, he'd not been able to deny himself a little satisfaction.

Opportunity…

Yeah, who would have thought getting mugged would turn out to be the perfect occasion to get closer to the woman who both owned and rejected his heart.

A poetic irony if he'd ever heard one.

Completing the last thought, he let his mind drift back to the mugging, when he'd been down on the ground and one of the men had been rifling through his clothing. Not to take anything, he knew, so why? To leave something? There had been that sound like paper crinkling…

He quickly checked his pockets. His fingers nicked something foreign, something that crinkled now. He latched onto it, pulled the sheet free, unfolded it, and smoothed out its wrinkles.

Then he strained against the low light to read the penciled missive.

Following the Cowboy Code
by the Cowboy Poet

A man not following the Cowboy Code
puts himself on a dangerous road.
This time you've been warned, next time you'll
be mourned.

His heart kick started again for a reason very different from the last. The Cowboy Poet sounded serious. Could the poet have been one of the men who had attacked him?

Chance didn't like the way things were stacking up against him. Maybe he'd better move on.

*Now.*

Dear Lord, what would Pru think then? he wondered. That he'd stopped back so he could get a quick thrill with her? She'd never forgive him.

He was thinking on it when he heard a strange noise. Kind of a…chirping.

*There it was again!* Head still throbbing from where it had been whacked, Chance sat upright and looked around the room.

Another noise…this time a high-pitched shriek.

Realizing the sound had come from a box on one of the nightstands—an intercom?—he rolled over to get a better look. A fancy handwriting on the unit identified it as a Baby Safe monitor.

"M'ma!" came a squeal, making him start.

''Squirt...''

Grinning again, Chance rolled off the bed and moved to the doorway where he heard more noises coming from the next room just down the hall. Drawn to them like they were a siren call, he tiptoed to the next door and opened it a crack, only to see the red-haired toddler he'd met earlier standing in her crib.

The room was dimly lit by a lamp on the chest of drawers. It was kind of an unusual find in a girl's room—a cowboy on a bucking bronc.

''Hey, Squirt, aren't you supposed to be sleeping?'' he asked in a soothing voice so as not to scare her.

Rather than being scared, the toddler shrieked in delight when she saw him. A big smile beamed from her small face, reminding him of someone other than Justine. Mitch, he supposed.

Chase approached the crib. The little girl wore footed pajamas imprinted with mustangs. Her dark-red hair poked out in every direction. She looked like a bizarre little rodeo clown—the cutest he'd ever seen.

''Hope up!'' she demanded, raising her arms to him.

''You shouldn't take to strangers so readily,'' he scolded her, even as he couldn't resist complying. He sauntered to her crib, asking, ''Didn't your mama ever tell you not to talk to strangers?''

A bubble escaped her mouth as she made a rude noise at him, then with both hands slapped at the crib's bar holding her hostage.

''What's that you say?'' Chance asked, giving her an expression of surprise that seemed to delight her.

"You say I'm not a stranger because we already met? Well then, that's different."

Chance freed Hope from the crib and fitted her to his hip, then rubbed the small of her back soothingly with his free hand. She reached out and tugged at the loose hair on his shoulder, then touched his face.

"Cheek!" she jabbered, clearly enough so he understood. "Nose." One finger touched the tip.

"Oh, yeah? Then where's my mouth?" he asked.

When she moved her finger to show him, he took it between his lips. "Mmm."

Her blue eyes were wide on his for a moment. Then her forehead suddenly wrinkled and she cried, "M'ma!"

"Hungry, huh?"

Chance didn't have a clue if a kid this age was supposed to eat in the middle of the night or not. He intended to find Pru and ask her, but she was already there, transfixed in the doorway, wearing an expression akin to horror.

"What are you doing in here?"

"I didn't wake her, I swear. I heard her prattling on that baby monitor. Why is that thing in *your* room, anyhow?"

"Because her room is next to mine, of course," Pru quickly said. "You know I've always helped take care of the girls."

"Oh."

"M'ma!" Hope twisted away from Chance and held her arms out to Pru.

Pru reached for the little girl and Chance gave her over, wondering at the odd sense of dissatisfaction he felt when he was free of her.

"She's hungry—right, Squirt?" He stroked a couple of dark-red tufts down in place on her head. "So we were about to find Aunt Pru to get her some food."

"Aunt Pru will take care of her after you leave."

Chance couldn't mistake the tension in her voice. She was still miffed with him for weakening her resolve to keep him at arm's length, he decided.

"I didn't know I was going anywhere."

"You are. *Where* is up to you." She couldn't even look him in the eye. "But you can't stay here now. Hope would have slept straight through if you hadn't..."

Chance couldn't resist raising his eyebrows and asking, "If I hadn't what?"

Pru got tight-lipped all of a sudden, and she gave him a filthy look that tickled him.

"Made so much noise?" he added, when they both knew she was the one who'd been doing all the hollering.

Hope started babbling again, and Pru shifted her, giving him the evil eye. "If you're trying to embarrass me, you're succeeding, okay?"

"No, Prunella, no." His heart fell. "There's no reason to be embarrassed. Not with me. Not ever. If I made you feel that way, I'm sorry. You believe me, don't you?"

Hesitating, she finally nodded.

"Good." He cupped her cheek with one hand, and when Hope squirmed, rubbed her back with the other. "So, where's that ice pack?"

"Let me put Hope down, and I'll get it for you."

Chance watched Pru as she set Hope back in the crib and kissed the little girl's forehead.

"You go back to sleep like a good girl," Pru murmured, petting Hope's head.

A disbelieving Chance watched as Hope yawned and her big blue eyes grew smaller as her lids flickered and lowered. She babbled something too low for him to catch, and Pru whispered to her in return.

The sight of them so close made Chance yearn for something he'd never defined before.

Pru as a mother, fussing over his child...

Could it ever happen?

More important—*should* it?

Not every mother ran away, leaving her husband and child brokenhearted, Chance told himself.

Still, he shook away the whole notion as foolishness. If he left town now, he'd never get another shot with Pru—he just knew that in his gut—so he steeled himself from wanting something else he'd never be allowed to have.

Pru touched Hope's forehead one last time and backed off. Without speaking, she indicated he should lead the way out into the hallway.

Brushing by him, she murmured, "Let's get you that ice pack."

Back in the bedroom where she'd left it, she had Chance sit down and hold the cold pack to the lump she'd found on the back of his head, while she finished what he'd interrupted earlier. She applied something to his cut lip that stung like hell, but Chance was done playing helpless.

Wondering if Pru realized he'd recovered a lot faster than he'd let on, he savored their final moments of closeness. Who knew if there would be others?

When she examined the contusions on his chest, and especially the darkening area of his solar plexus where he'd been kicked, she murmured, "I'd feel a lot better if you'd get your ribs X-rayed."

"I feel better just knowing you care."

"It's professional—"

"What about that?" he quickly cut in, hoping to distract her from what had happened to him. "How come you're waitressing instead of nursing like you always wanted?"

The best thing he could do was to put Pru on the defensive. Besides, he really wanted to know.

"Life got in the way" was all she would say. Then she turned the tables on him. "Chance, what does the poem mean?"

His pulse skittered. "What poem?"

From her jeans pocket, she withdrew the folded missive. "I found this on the bed when I came back with the cold pack."

Not wanting to alarm her, he took the warning from her fingers and, securing it in his own pocket, drawled, "Just something I was playing around with—"

"You don't write poetry!" she snapped, expression concerned. "This has something to do with the men who attacked you, doesn't it?"

"Forget about it, Pru. It's over."

"Not according to that message. What is this Cowboy Code it talks about, Chance?" she asked, her voice tight. "What is it that you've done?"

*What had he done?*

Of course what happened to him had to be his own fault, something *he'd* instigated, he thought angrily. Disappointed that Pru didn't think better of him, Chance suddenly itched to leave. Standing, he grabbed his shirt and drew it on.

"I'd better get back to the Curly-Q."

"Chance, please…"

"Think what you want about me, Pru. People always do." Rather, his father and brothers always had. He'd never tried to disabuse them of their notions about him being a bad seed. "I'm used to it."

"I didn't mean it like that. I think you're in some kind of trouble and could use some help. Bart—"

"Don't go bringing Saint Bart in on this."

"But, Chance—"

"Promise me, Pru."

She tried that evil-eye stuff on him again, but this time it didn't work. Closed off from the closeness they had just shared, Chance stared back without flinching. It became a test of wills, and for once he won.

"All right," she finally said, looking worried rather than angry. "I promise I won't say anything to Bart."

"Good."

"But I hope you'll change your mind and go to him. He *is* your brother and he *does* care what happens to you."

"You'd think so, wouldn't you?"

She just shook her head at him.

Fighting the urge to kiss Pru one last time, Chance turned to go. Then he froze in the doorway. He couldn't leave it like this, not without warning her.

"Pru," he said without turning to face her. He couldn't face her, didn't want to see her anger and disapproval. "I want you to know that if I have to leave suddenly, it has nothing to do with you. It's not us that's driving me away."

He could feel her eyes digging into his back as she calmly said, ''There is no us.''

''Yeah, Pru, there is,'' he argued. ''In your heart you know it, and so do I. You're the only woman I've ever loved, Prunella Prescott, and, God willing, I'll always come back to you.''

# Chapter Six

*God willing, I'll always come back to you...*

That something was desperately wrong and Chance wouldn't tell her was driving Pru crazy enough to pace circles around her bedroom at the crack of dawn.

She'd barely slept all night.

Throwing herself back on the unmade bed, she caught Chance's scent, then found the Stetson he'd dropped on the floor. Holding it, she closed her eyes and breathed deep, tried to banish from her mind the horror she'd felt after he'd left. She didn't know how long she stood at the door, wanting to scream.

Chance Quarrels had done it to her again—he'd fooled her into thinking he cared, and now he was going to ditch her the way he had last time.

Even as she made the mental indictment, something in her denied it.

He wasn't walking out of her life without her knowing—this time he'd given her fair warning. This time she didn't think he wanted to go.

And it had something to do with that Cowboy Code warning, she was certain.

*...next time you'll be mourned...*

That sounded as if someone was planning on killing Chance if he didn't do what was expected of him, Pru thought. But what could that be?

Double damnation! Why had she promised not to say anything to Bart? A former lawman, his brother would surely know how to handle the situation…whatever it was. Not knowing was a problem in and of itself.

When was Chance going to get over this thing with his brothers? When would he get over his sense of abandonment over his mother walking out on them all? When were the Quarrels men—starting with old Emmett—going to grow up? she wondered, aware that her pulse was surging with misspent emotion.

Anger would get her nowhere, Pru decided. It would only cloud her mind and keep her from thinking straight. She took a couple of deep, calming breaths.

What she needed to be was crafty, so that she could find out what was going on and maybe do something about it. Okay, so she couldn't talk to Bart…but Chance hadn't made her promise not to talk to anyone else about his situation….

Pru showered and dressed and entered Hope's room. The toddler was already awake.

"Hi, cookie, did you have a good sleep?"

The blue eyes she'd inherited from Chance wide, Hope nodded.

"Did you have sweet dreams?"

Another nod.

"What did you dream about?"

"'Orses."

"Horses. Cowboys, too?" Pru asked, thinking of Chance.

"Yeah!"

"So what colors were the horses?"

This was a ritual they observed every morning. Pru assumed her daughter did dream, but she had no idea if Hope actually remembered anything specific. But questioning her about it was a way to get her reticent child to verbalize more, though many of Hope's words only she and Pru understood.

Chance seemed to understand his daughter, as well, she realized...

Cleaning and dressing Hope, Pru continued to encourage Hope's jabbering. Then she led her out to the kitchen, where she was pleased to see Justine already up and at the stove, making breakfast.

"Hey, Sis," Pru said, placing the toddler in a high chair. "Do you think you could feed Hope for me this morning?"

"Yeah, sure." Justine glanced over her shoulder. "Going somewhere?"

"Alcina's. I need to talk to her."

"About Chance?"

Was she that transparent? "Maybe."

Back still to Pru, Justine said, "I heard the two of you last night."

Heat suffused Pru's cheeks. Had anyone *not* heard? "Sorry if we disturbed you."

"I'm not worried about being disturbed, I'm worried about you." Her sister stopped what she was doing and faced her. "Anything you care to talk about?"

"Maybe later."

"I'll hold you to that."

Pru knew Justine would, too. She and her sister were as close as any two siblings could be, and they were both equally close to their parents.

If only Chance knew what it felt like to have a loving and stable relationship with even one member of his family, she thought wistfully, then everything between them might be different.

He would be different.

And trouble wouldn't have followed him back to Silver Springs....

JUST BEFORE DAWN Emmett rose in a fine mood, knowing exactly where his youngest had been until the wee hours of the morning, when he'd heard the boy's motorcycle roar past the house. Prudence Prescott would make a fine daughter-in-law, he'd long ago decided. More to the point, if Chance and Pru were together, she would finally admit that little Hope was his grandchild as he'd suspected from the first.

Emmett was no fool.

He knew how long and how much that girl had loved his boy. And she'd been raised right by her parents, even if she had gone against her preacher father's teachings and succumbed to Chance's physical charms.

Emmett couldn't see her going off with another man, not by a long shot.

He wondered if Chance had it figured out yet.

Not that Emmett would dare say what he thought—that Chance ought to make an honest woman of Pru and settle down to take care of little Hope and give her some brothers and sisters.

If he got himself involved he might just drive his

son away—the last thing he needed right now. Chance might not be the most reliable of his boys, but he was of great help when he put his mind to it.

And he could change into something better, more reliable, given the right incentive, like a family of his own.

So he'd have to think on it, Emmett decided, a grin tearing at his lips. He'd have to devise a way to subtly push them closer together....

After finishing his morning ablutions, he entered his office and made himself comfortable in the leather high-backed chair behind his desk. And after opening the hand-carved cigar box that held more than met the eye, he pulled out a fine cigar and trimmed the tip.

Damn shame when a grown man had to smoke in secret.

A man had to do what a man had to do, Emmett reminded himself, even if it meant hoodwinking his own blood into doing what needed to be done, as well. He lit up and took a couple of satisfying puffs before the telephone rang.

His heart stuttered, and sudden heat flooded him. By the second ring he already had a sweaty hand wrapped around the receiver so no one else would beat him to it.

Expectation sharpening his tone when he answered, he merely said, "Curly-Q!"

"Mr. Emmett Quarrels, please."

The sultry-voiced request raised the hairs on his arms to attention. Which realty company would she be from? he wondered, now certain that Frank Ewing's "accident" hadn't been an accident at all, since

he got a call like this after every bad-luck incident
on the place.

"You're speakin' to him, honey."

Not seeming to note his darkening tone, she said,
"Wonderful! This is Julia Hernandez from Juniper
Realty. Mr. Quarrels, I understand you're looking to
put the Curly-Q on the market and I—"

"Who gave you that information?"

"Why...your son."

"Which one?" he demanded.

"Mr. Quarrels...um...is there a problem?"

*"Which son?"*

"Actually, I don't know," she admitted, now
sounding a bit tentative. "The message was on my
machine when I got in late last night. The man didn't
actually leave his name...just yours."

"And what did he say exactly?"

Her hesitation didn't last long.

"Why, that you were ready to divest yourself of
a ranch that had become too problematic for you to
handle anymore."

Streaks of light were barely limning the horizon.
"And you couldn't wait until a decent hour to make
a deal?" A new day was breaking but he was feeling
older than ever.

"He specifically said to call this early if I didn't
want to be part of a stampede on your property."

"There won't be no stampede," Emmett informed
her more calmly than he was feeling. "Because the
Curly-Q is not for sale!"

There was a short silence.

Then the realty agent seemed to gather herself together just fine, because she said, "I know how you
must feel about a place where you've lived for so

many years.'' She added just the proper amount of concern in her tone. ''But I think your son must agree that the Golden Years were meant to be enjoyed and—''

Emmett cut off her prattle by slamming down the receiver. He waited for his pulse to settle.

It had taken a while and lots of bad luck incidents for him to believe that someone was out to destroy him if he didn't sell the ranch. That was why he'd called his sons. Had he been honest with them, he doubted they would have agreed to come home. He'd figured having them around would get the Curly-Q back on its financial feet and that would put a stop to all this nonsense.

But Barton had been back for nearly a month now, and the bad luck was continuing, one incident after another, despite the presence of a bona fide lawman on the spread…albeit one who didn't know the truth.

Money had become shorter than short. The mortgage payment was more than a year overdue. And his former partner, banker Tucker Dale, was threatening him with foreclosure if he couldn't come up with the money soon.

If that happened, everything he'd worked his whole life for would be lost. His family legacy would be gone forever, after everything he had done for the area—he and the two other men who, nearly five decades ago, had pumped life into the old town and mine. Some people still recalled Tucker, he guessed, since the banker had held on until a dozen or so years ago when he'd moved over to Taos, but Noah Warner was a distant memory, even to him.

And if a man was remembered by what he left behind, then he, too, was destined to be forgotten,

Emmett reasoned, if he let whoever was trying to destroy him—to wrest the Curly-Q from him—win. Normally he was a player. But fighting an invisible enemy wasn't his best suit, especially when he didn't know *why* the spread was so important to someone else.

That's what he had to figure out…*why!*

Until then he could only pray there was a way out of the disaster that seemed ready to strike them all.

HAVING GOTTEN A GOOD LOOK at himself in the mirror when he'd tried to shave his bruised and swollen face, Chance was under no illusions that he could hide what had happened the night before. And though he should've been ready for his father and brother's reactions when he entered the main house for breakfast, he wasn't.

Saint Bart and Pa were in some kind of confab just outside the dining room. But they both stopped to gape at him.

"What kind of a fix did you get yourself into this time?" Bart asked.

Defensive, Chance growled, "What does it look like?" yet hoped for the best.

"Like you ran into a brick wall," Emmett said. "Or a couple of brick fists."

"Still getting into fights?" Bart went on. "I was hoping you could set an example for my kids."

Chance glanced at Daniel, who was just coming from his room, leading with a great-looking shiner. "Seems to me you already took care of that."

Obviously realizing that all was not well, his nephew gave them an alarmed expression, detoured behind them and disappeared fast.

As usual, his family assumed whatever happened to him was his fault, Chance groused to himself. He wondered how Bart would feel if no one ever gave *him* the benefit of doubt. But, of course, that would never happen.

Saint Bart couldn't make a wrong move.

Let them think what they would, Chance decided—he wasn't about to enlighten them.

Instead, he changed the subject. "Has the new hand turned up yet?"

Bart started. "What new hand?"

"I hired a day worker by the name of Kleef Hatsfield and told him to show up first thing this morning."

"What call did *you* have to do any such thing?" Bart demanded.

"I'm part of this family corporation, aren't I?" Chance demanded. "One of our men is down. We needed help. I got us some."

To Chance's surprise, Pa said, "Good."

But Bart couldn't see his way to be gracious. "This Hatsfield better be worth something."

"If he isn't, I'm sure you won't have any trouble telling us all about it."

Chance brushed by them and into the dining room where he meant to give Felice his apologies for skipping out on dinner. He wasn't about to let Bart and Pa get to him enough to miss out on another of her meals.

Working under the wagon wheel chandelier that hung over the big pine table, the center of which was decorated with ivory candles and dried flowers of the region, an uncommonly sullen-looking Lainey was depositing flatware alongside the breakfast plates.

Lord, how she'd grown!

"Hmm, I don't believe we've met, miss," he teased. "Though you do look somewhat familiar."

"Uncle Chance!"

Lainey brightened for a moment, then, as if remembering herself, sank back into that dour stance. In the old days she would have launched herself at him, and no matter how big she had grown, he would gladly have picked her up and twirled her around the way he had since she was a toddler. Instead she stood there, apparently all torn up inside.

"Looks like you woke up on the wrong side of bed this morning."

"Just the wrong bed." Lainey set down the last of the flatware. "As in, *not mine*."

Obviously she wasn't any happier being here this time than he was.

"Tough move, huh?"

"It was bad enough losing...never mind."

Chance knew she was thinking about losing her mother. Now *that* he could relate to. He put an arm around her shoulder and gave it a squeeze.

"Hey, if this place gets to you too bad, come see me, okay?"

Lainey nodded and another smile trembled on her lips. "Dad just doesn't understand."

Saint Bart didn't understand a lot of things—not that Chance would tell her that. He would never purposely come between his brother and his kids.

"Well, I sure will try," he said.

"Thanks, Uncle Chance. I can always count on you."

At least someone could, he thought, his heart softening toward his niece, wanting to erase her pain.

Knowing her mom had been teaching her how to use a real camera and lenses, he said, "So tell me how your photography is coming."

At last lightening up, Lainey said, "Great. I'm getting pretty good at it. I've been taking pictures around the ranch and putting together an album just like Mom and I used to do together."

Now there was the happy niece he remembered, Chance thought with satisfaction.

It gave him a weird feeling, his brother's kids both turning to him as if maybe he had some answers for them, when—not having a kid of his own—he didn't even know the damn questions!

"WHEN IT COMES to Chance Quarrels, I don't have any answers for you, Pru," Alcina said from the counter, where she was busy arranging strawberries onto individual plates of fruit salad. "He's never been what you would call open about himself. But no one knows that better than you."

Pru watched her friend work. As owner of the Silver Springs Bed and Breakfast, the only place in town to rent a room, Alcina took pride in her gourmet breakfasts for her customers. The kitchen was filled with the odor of homemade blueberry muffins—minus the one Pru had snatched and practically inhaled the moment she'd walked in.

"So how am I going to find out what's going on?" Pru mused just as the door between kitchen and dining room swung open. "You should have seen him, his beautiful face all swollen and bloody..."

"Sounds horrible." Josie Walker entered the kitchen, tangled light-brown, shoulder-length hair spilling from below her Stetson. She wore jeans ripped at the knees, a denim jacket over a white T-shirt and a belt with a fancy silver buckle inscribed with her initials. "Who are we talking about?"

A cat practically sat on one of her disreputable boots. Its little white face and almond-shaped blue eyes were edged by soft gray ears and a gray chin.

"Chance Quarrels."

"I heard the prodigal son returned." Josie filched a blueberry muffin from the pan and grabbed a big mug. "I guess I'll meet him at work today." She poured her own coffee and took a slug. "Ah, now I can wake up."

Pru had met Josie at Alcina's before and knew the woman was the Curly-Q wrangler, had almost been killed by her ex-husband and was now Bart Quarrels's woman. Josie still lived at Alcina's, having graduated from the tiny ironing room to one of the fancy guest suites. Alcina had confided that Josie was spending more on that suite than she made working with the Curly-Q horses—a top rodeo barrel racer, she had won and saved a tidy sum over the past few years.

Pru said, "Chance got himself beat up last night."

Josie nearly choked on her bite of muffin. "Uh-oh. On his first day back? Who—"

"That's what we're trying to figure out."

"He won't even tell *me*," Pru added.

"Hmm. Maybe I could get the lowdown."

Pru brightened. "You must know him from the rodeo circuit—well enough that he'd confide in you?"

"More like know of him." Josie broke off a tiny bit of muffin and gave it to the cat. "We've crossed paths a few times, that's all."

"Then how—"

"Will 'Billy-Boy' Spencer is how. He used to be an All-Around contender," she said, referring to the men who competed in all three rough-stock competitions—saddle bronc, bareback and bull riding. "Now he's working for the Curly-Q, too. I know him…he knows Chance. Simple."

She took another bit of muffin and washed it down with coffee.

"Oh-h, that's sneaky," Pru said. "But I like it. You'd really do that for me?"

"For another woman who loves a Quarrels man enough to fight for him?" Josie nodded. "You bet."

"Speaking of that…you and Bart…how are things going?" Pru asked.

Josie's angular face lit, the smile softening it, making her look downright pretty. "We're doing just fine, thank you very much."

"Anything permanent in the air?"

"That's the plan. We're just playing it slow on account of his kids."

"They have a problem with you?"

"They have a problem with their mother dying and their being moved away from their school and their friends and everything they know." The cat was twirling around her ankles, so she bent over and picked it up. "Come here, Miss Kitty." She kissed the cat's nose.

"Kids are pretty smart," Pru said, thinking of Hope.

"You're right. And Bart wanted to tell Daniel and Lainey about us, but I talked him into waiting—I mean, they know we're seeing each other, but not how serious. It just wouldn't be fair to spring another major life change on them so fast. They like me okay, and I want to keep it like that. So we're trying to do this slow and smart.''

"Loving a Quarrels man isn't easy, is it?" Pru asked, looking to Alcina, who was setting the plates of fruit on an antique silver tray.

The blonde ignored the probe. "I need to take care of my guests."

Pru watched her set a spray of flowers along the plates. Alcina made everything she touched look special.

"And I'd better get to work or the boss'll have my hide," Josie announced, setting down the cat and grabbing a muffin to go.

"I think he already has that," Alcina said with an unladylike snort.

The three women looked at each other and burst out laughing.

And Pru left Alcina's a few minutes later feeling a whole lot better than when she had arrived.

If Chance really was in serious trouble, she had in Alcina and Josie two allies who would go the mat to help her get him back out of it.

# Chapter Seven

Moving cows was a perfect way to get back to nature, to let the world slow down for a bit and to forget about the problems that seemed to have followed him from the civilized world. No matter that he didn't fancy himself a real rancher, Chance enjoyed being out on the range and sitting a long-legged horse with an easy gait.

He was riding a gelding Appaloosa named Predator, who evidently got his kicks from making the stocky animals and their progeny move their hides faster. The moment that gelding spotted the cows, he neighed, pricked up his ears and hoofed it straight over to the ladies. The cows reacted symbiotically to Predator and his cohorts—each animal knowing its place in the chain. The beast-to-beast dance began immediately—cows running, horses and dogs pursuing.

As if it were a race and they didn't know the fix was already in...

Predator had more energy than he could burn, Chance decided—the horse was keeping him fully awake and sharp in the saddle. Josie had told him the gelding was a handful. The Curly-Q's wrangler did know her horses.

And her man.

Saint Bart was besotted and couldn't hide his tender feelings for the woman, who was on the scrawny side and a little faded for Chance's taste. He preferred ripe redheads, he thought, a snippet of the night's encounter with Pru coming back to him.

He shifted in the saddle and forced his mind back where it belonged—on the range.

Chance did recognize Josie as a hotshot barrel racer. He'd met her once or twice but couldn't say he knew her. Though, apparently she knew Will, because they'd had their heads together a spell before saddling up. Josie had come along for the ride, mostly sticking near Bart.

Chance watched his brother and his woman every now and then, wondering what it would be like for him and Pru to be working at a common goal.

Not that today's mission was a big one.

They—him, Bart, Josie, Will and Kleef Hatsfield, who'd shown up halfway through breakfast—were moving the part of the herd that had been grazing in the southwest pasture. In disgrace with his father because of his suspension from school, Daniel had been left behind. The objective was to narrow the grazing lands as bad weather approached. That way it wouldn't take as much time to supplement the herd's feed or take as much work to get those calves to the weighing house and pens if and when Bart deemed it necessary.

Halfway through the morning Will came alongside Chance, who slowed the gelding, though Predator fought the bit.

"They're in the rhythm now."

"An easy drive," Chance agreed.

They rode side by side for a few minutes before Will asked, "Need any help looking over your shoulder?"

Chance knew Will was referring to his bruises, and the offer came from the camaraderie of rodeoing together.

"I've always done pretty well on my own."

"Took you by surprise, though, right?" Will said. "So who around here has a grudge against you?"

"I wouldn't know," Chance said truthfully.

"You don't know who rearranged your face?"

"Not even a guess." He attempted a grin, but his split lip hurt too much and the would-be smile turned into a grimace. "Two men with masks on a street with no lights pretty much keeps a man in the dark."

"I've heard some rumors about you," Will said tentatively.

"You believe everything you hear?"

"Depends. It's always interesting to hear both sides of a story, though."

That Will seemed to accept his word without making a judgment call put Chance at ease.

"Let's say I got involved in a lose-lose situation," he admitted, not intending to go into details, even to a sympathetic ear. "A man lost his life because of me."

Thoughtful for a moment, Will reasonably said, "Sounds like you're blaming yourself for something that maybe you couldn't help."

"I made a bad decision, and that's on my head," Chance argued. "That man's family will never have him back, but maybe they can get justice."

Will nodded. "Well, you change your mind about me watching your back, you just holler."

"I've got a good strong voice," Chance agreed, moving off to circle a stray.

As for Will's offer—Chance wasn't one to depend on others any more than he let them depend on him.

He got the cow and her calf back in with the herd and realized that Kleef Hatsfield was nearby, watching him instead of the cattle. He seemed to have some special interest, Chance thought, waving the cowboy off to assure him that he had everything in hand.

Kleef gathered his bay and shot him to the rear of the herd to ride drag, and Chance put it out of mind as he rejoined the drive.

Back to business....

A couple of truckloads of calves had already been shipped out to auction more than a week ago— Chance knew because Pa had told him—bringing in enough money to keep the spread operating, if not in the black. He had some thoughts on that...not that his notions would be appreciated by Pa or Bart.

Meanwhile, though they were pushing the herd in closer, he also knew that Bart was determined to winter all of them in the canyon if beef prices didn't climb soon.

And Chance couldn't help but wonder how Reed would handle the situation.

Reed was the *real* rancher—always had been— albeit he was running someone else's spread for the time being. Or maybe permanently, for all they knew. Pa maintained his middle son would be along any day now, but Chance wasn't yet convinced.

Would Reed really be content to once more take

a back seat to their older brother, a professed lawman at heart?

A lawman...

Bart would be the one to talk to about the threats against him, Chance knew, but he didn't want help from a man who disrespected and maybe disliked him, even if that man was his own brother.

He would have to handle this on his own, as always.

So, as he worked, he set his mind to remembering every detail that he could dredge up from the attack.

Two men, masked...two against one...not good odds when he didn't know his enemy.

Riding on automatic, Chance went over every punch, starting with the one that had split open his lip. Something hard beyond knuckles had smacked him in the mouth—a ring by the feel of it, and one that had some bulk.

And then he remembered the shocks that had stunned him. A tazer?

Somehow Chance didn't think that he would have gotten to his feet so quickly if he'd been shocked with a real weapon; the jolts would have been more powerful, possibly knocking him out altogether. Besides which, he reasoned, a cattle prod was more likely, since one would be commonly available in the area.

The men were obviously trying to scare him into forgetting what he knew.

What he didn't know was...how far were they willing to go to erase his memory?

FINGERING THE STETSON that Chance had forgotten in her room when he'd left the night before, Pru rode out to the range with Moon-Eye in his rusty pickup. The old hand was hauling a simple lunch that Felice had pulled together for the crew—roast beef sandwiches, potato salad and lemonade.

She could have left the hat at the house, but she wanted to see for herself that he was all right. And she meant to find out if Josie had learned anything new about the attack.

"Hang on," Moon-Eye instructed. "It's gonna get a little bumpy along here."

Jouncing over rock, Pru said, "How much far-r-th-ther?"

"Just ahead some."

Which turned out to be another five minutes of physical punishment.

But then they came off the rock pile and onto the comparatively flat earthen floor of the canyon. There they sidled along Silverado Creek, which rushed several yards below for nearly another mile, before they reached the appointed rest stop. This was a low area with a gentle incline, affording the stock easy access to the water that they would be required to cross. Pru had never been so glad to get out of a vehicle in her life.

Josie and a good-looking cowboy—Will?—sat in the shade of a cottonwood near the creek. Beyond, cows and their calves grazed or closed in on the water source for a drink. The sun glared in her eyes as she searched in vain for Chance.

When she didn't see him, she left his hat in the passenger seat and moved toward the cottonwood just as Bart rode up and dismounted. Securing his horse's reins to a cedar, he strode toward the pickup and her, the ranch dogs at his heels.

"Pru, what a surprise."

"Bart."

His expression speculative, he didn't bother to ask what she was doing there. Of course he knew it had to do with his brother. He passed her by and helped Moon-Eye set out the eats along the rear of the pickup bed.

Anxious to find out what she could before Chance interrupted, Pru headed straight for Josie and the man, who indeed turned out to be Will. He was another looker—she couldn't miss the fair hair, light-brown eyes or the cocky way he gave her a once-over.

"Sorry to disappoint you, Pru," Josie began, "but Will couldn't get the story out of Chance, either."

Pru's heart fell. "Nothing?"

"Nothing straight," Will admitted. "And I gave it my best shot without being too obvious."

"So what *did* you find out?"

"I asked him about the rumors making the rodeo circuit. Word is…well, it seems he's in real trouble and is hiding out here."

A fist in Pru's middle made continuing difficult. "What kind of trouble?" she choked out, thinking at the same time that maybe she'd be better off not knowing.

Will was clearly uncomfortable. "I hate telling tales out of school."

"Please, Will, anything might help," Josie said. "You saw what those men did to him."

"And I offered to watch his back," Will assured them, "but he turned me down. I expect he doesn't want to involve anyone else."

Getting more frustrated by the second, Pru asked, "Involve us in what?"

"Bank robbery."

Certainly not what Pru had hoped to hear. Knees weak, she leaned back against the tree trunk. "Are you saying that Chance was involved in a felony?"

"I'm not saying any such thing," Will told her. "Not for sure. It's a rumor, is all. The two robbers were captured, but word is there's a third man involved—the brains behind the operation."

"And you think that might be Chance."

Now Will was becoming agitated. "I didn't say that. I asked for his side of the story, but all he did was dance around it some. He said he was in a no-win situation..." Appearing torn, Will finished, "And he admitted that a man died because of him."

Josie gasped, "Oh, no!"

Shocked, Pru didn't know how to respond. She pressed her hands hard into the tree bark until it bit into her fingertips. Her mouth opened in protest, but nothing came out. The word *murder* stuck in her throat.

"Take it easy, Pru," Josie said softly, her expression concerned. "Sometimes things aren't what they seem."

"She's right," Will piped in with what seemed to be forced confidence. "You got to get the whole story before you can draw any conclusions. What I think is that Chance is blaming himself for something he couldn't do nothin' about."

*But a man had died and he blamed himself...*

Pru didn't know what to think. It was all she could do to keep from crying with the knowledge. The backs of her eyelids stung, and a lump settled in the middle of her throat.

"Listen, if you get wind of anything more—either of you—you'll tell me, right?"

"Sure thing," Will promised.

"And maybe I'll work on Chance myself," Josie offered. "See what I can find out. My guess is he didn't have anything to do with that death, Pru, not directly. Maybe it was some kind of accident."

"I hope you're right."

"A person who is willing to kill another—or even to let someone die—has real evil in him," Josie assured her. "I've had firsthand experience with that kind of darkness in a person—my late ex-husband tried to kill me more than once. But I don't feel that darkness in Chance, Pru, and I think I would recognize it."

Getting hold of herself, Pru swallowed past the lump in her throat and nodded. "You're right. Chance isn't evil. He's not. Thanks."

Though why she was offering thanks for bad news, Pru couldn't say. And she also didn't know why she was leaving this to two people who were virtual strangers to her. Maybe what she needed to do was ask Chance directly what happened. Wear him down until he *had* to tell her. But even thinking about doing so made her vocal cords squeeze tight and her mouth go dry as cotton.

Moon-Eye called them to chow just as she saw Chance riding up on an Appaloosa.

With his face all busted up, he looked as terrible as she felt inside.

What in the world had he gotten himself into? Pru asked herself. And what did that Cowboy Code warning mean? She didn't want to do any more speculating. She wanted the truth.

Chance Quarrels was a good man—she believed that as deeply as she believed in Heaven. But he must have gotten himself suckered into something he shouldn't have, by hanging out with rodeo drifters.

Even so…a bank robbery…a man killed…

Dear Lord, she couldn't fathom how he could have come to this.

"PRUNELLA, WHAT'S WRONG?" Chance asked as he approached her. He'd seen her right off when he'd dismounted. But now, up close, he could swear she was holding herself from crying. Concerned, he stepped closer. "Are you okay?"

"Yes…no, I'm not." Shaking her head, she backed off. "Listen, we have to talk, Chance." A note of desperation threaded her words. "Now!"

He wanted to touch her, to take her in his arms and tell her that everything would be okay, but that might make things worse. So he kept his distance and watched her face closely.

"Okay, so talk."

"Alone!" she insisted.

He glanced around him. Others were in earshot. Will was watching them until he realized Chance noticed. Then the cowboy turned his attention back to the grub he'd just gotten.

"Have you eaten?" he asked Pru.

"I'm not hungry. But get yourself something, and I'll find a place for us to sit away from the others."

Trying not to draw conclusions before he heard what she had to say—which is what his family did to him every time he turned around—Chance nodded and strode over to Moon-Eye's pickup, at present turned into the contemporary version of a chuck wagon. He grabbed a paper plate and plopped a sandwich and a mound of potato salad on it.

Coming alongside him, Bart asked, "Where's Hatsfield?"

Chance glanced around. "Not here, I guess."

"I wouldn't be asking if he was, now, would I?"

"Do you know the meaning of the word *rhetorical?*" Chance muttered.

He turned his back on his aggravating brother to pour himself a big glass of lemonade. He hadn't seen Kleef in a while. Not since the man had shadowed him earlier that morning. Surely the new hired hand hadn't gotten himself lost. That's all he'd need.

Then Saint Bart would be on his back.

"Maybe he's just picking up a stray or two," Chance suggested as he went in search of Pru.

She sat in the shade of a cottonwood away from the others. Chance plopped himself down a few yards from her, fearing he knew what she would say—that what happened between them the night before was a mistake that shouldn't be repeated. Maybe she was right. Maybe he ought to leave her be for her own good.

And maybe he would, if the thought didn't leave him empty inside.

"So talk," he said again.

"Why are you back, Chance? Why did you come back *now?*"

"Pa needed help—"

"No, really."

"Just because we don't get along all the time—"

"Chance, please!" Growing red, she lowered her

voice. "The truth, not an excuse...not the Curly-Q...not even me. The real reason."

"What are you getting at?"

"You're in trouble, aren't you?"

"Who said?"

"Who had to say—just look at you! What have you gotten yourself involved in, Chance? What have you done?"

Trying to ignore what sounded like an accusation, he said, "Just calm down, Prunella."

"Don't Prunella me! I know about the rumors, Chance." Catching herself, she took a deep breath and lowered her voice. "About how you might have been involved in a bank robbery. About how a man died..."

Her expression reflected the anguish Chance was feeling inside. "If you know it all, then you don't need me to confirm it, do you?"

"Chance, please—"

"No! You have it all sorted out in your head, so you just think what you want!" Chance yelled, suddenly feeling as if he were about to explode. Suddenly everyone was plaguing him with speculations. "I am the bad seed, after all! Just ask anyone around here!"

All eyes were on them.

Furious and heartbroken that Pru of all people would think the worst of him, Chance stomped off toward the horses where Kleef Hatsfield was tying up his mount.

"We got a problem?" Kleef asked.

"Nothing to concern you."

Throwing himself up on Predator, he rode off, cutting straight through the herd. The already-edgy cows parted, giving him a clear path.

Why couldn't Pru have left it alone?

Why couldn't he have confided in her? a voice countered. Because he was ashamed and guilt ridden and hadn't wanted to see her disappointment in him.

But now he'd seen worse.

Chance rode Predator fast uphill for several minutes before coming to his senses and slowing. The gelding had worked hard all morning and was now foaming at the mouth.

"Sorry, boy, I shouldn't be taking it out on you."

He patted the horse's sweat-slicked neck and turned him around and eased him back down the incline. The land here rose over the creek fast and sharp, and a barbed-wire fence was strung along the ridge to keep the cows away from the edge. Part of the herd had drifted this way to graze, having spread out from where they'd stopped for lunch.

But now they stared at him with baleful eyes. And though he walked Predator carefully through the herd, they seemed agitated. Wired.

Another thing he could take the blame for, Chance told himself.

He mused on it until a loud blast from behind spooked him, Predator, who shot sideways, and the herd.

"What the hell...!"

Chance whirled around in the saddle as the animals started moving as if of one mind. But another blast from a second direction quickly scattered them.

He didn't have time to consider the source as a third blast sounded and all hell broke loose around him.

Stampede...and he was in the midst of it!

Chance didn't have to arouse Predator. A real cow horse, he was ready to do his stuff. Horse and rider veered to the left and quickly outdistanced the leaders. Using loud whistles and waving his coiled rope, he managed to turn the cows. He only prayed Bart and the others had been immediately alerted and were on their way.

Instinctively Chance pushed some nearby cows toward the creek to slow them—he figured the barbed wire fence and steep drop would stop them.

But the frantic beasts didn't stop.

A dozen or so broke through, trampling the barbed wire, hitting the incline too fast, sliding and skidding their way down to the water's edge. Calves bawled as they were pushed too fast by the bigger bodies surrounding them. He watched helplessly as a couple went down only to be trampled, their high-pitched screams of pain ringing in his ears.

He wasn't alone in this—Bart, Will, Josie and Kleef had all mounted and put up a block to the south. Even so, the remaining herd kept on, turning away from the humans, at a lower level than the ridge. The riders spread out in an effort to keep the herd together. Cows forged the creek at a safer crossing, slowing finally when they arrived on the other side.

They would soon stop, Chance thought, following. The area was laid out with electric fence. The wily cows wouldn't go near the tape that sat mere inches from the ground. Enough of them had experienced the pulsed current, which was strong enough to discourage animals from crossing it yet not strong enough to hurt them.

But the cows didn't stop, because there didn't seem to be a tape, Chance realized. Only when he got closer did he see that it lay flat on the ground. Though he took a quick look around for some cause, he saw nothing amiss.

On the other side of the downed fence, a calf lay struggling to rise. Chance figured the animal was finished and would have to be put down like the others at the ridge, but he decided to make certain. Maybe he could get the calf to its feet before more cows trampled it.

Dismounting fast, he dropped Predator's reins to the earth so the horse would stay put. He'd barely taken a step when he heard Bart yell his name.

"Chance! What the hell happened?"

He glanced back at his brother as he took another step, yelling, "This is one you can't blame me for!"

Too late he realized the electric fence tape lay directly below.

Expecting to be shocked, he tried to catch himself to no avail. He stumbled, and his boot went down hard, raising a cloud of red dust. And then he was caught by the searing agony of the electric shock that shot through his boot nails and up his leg, through his middle and out his shoulder.

He was thrown, his heart racing wildly before it plain stopped.

# Chapter Eight

"Chance!" Pru screamed as she watched him drop, the electric fence tape still caught behind his boot heel.

Having ridden straight through the creek behind the runaway herd with Moon-Eye, she was already opening the door before he could stop the pickup.

Will beat her to Chance by seconds and, using his Stetson, knocked the tape away from Chance's foot. It seemed to dance on its own.

"Damn!" Will cursed. "That wire's hot!"

Pru dropped to her knees, then felt for a pulse and put her cheek to Chance's lips. "He's not breathing! And his heart's not beating!"

Her reaction was instinctive—she administered a precordial thump on the chest in hopes of jump-starting his heart into beating again. But while his body responded involuntarily to the sharp blow, Chance remained inert.

Reality distorted for Pru.

The milling herd seemed to dissipate, and the humans gathering around her seemed giant in stature, as below her, the man she loved lay without a heartbeat.

*Dead!*

Panic filled her. "You can't be dead, Chance Quarrels, you can't die on me!"

A hand on her shoulder tried pulling her away. She shrugged it off and focused.

Quickly she slipped a hand behind his neck and tilted his head back to create an airway so she could give him mouth-to-mouth. Four quick breaths made his chest rise, filled his lungs with life-saving oxygen.

*No pulse.*

Repositioning herself, she ran her fingers over his ribs...found the right spot on the sternum...placed one palm over the other and pumped.

"One and two and three and..."

Fifteen strokes in all.

By the time she gave him two more breaths, Bart was down on the ground opposite her. "You breathe, I'll pump."

Knowing working as a team would be easier and more effective, Pru nodded.

They worked together in a kind of desperation that she had never before known—she who loved him and the brother who Chance didn't even believe cared.

"No pulse," Pru croaked.

"One...one thousand, two...one thousand, three... one thousand..."

Bart kept his strokes slow and steady, and she gave Chance a breath every fifth stroke.

*No pulse.*

A minute passed and still they worked over Chance.

*No pulse.*

And another…

Suddenly a flutter brushed her fingertips.

"Wait, I've got it!" Nearly strangling on her excitement, she put her face close to his lips and felt a faint warmth blossom along her cheek. "He's breathing!"

Then she broke down and sobbed in relief.

Bart quickly took over. "Will, get back to the house fast and call an ambulance!"

"I'm already gone," the hand said, practically flying onto his mount and heading back along the creek bed.

Josie helped Pru up as Bart got Moon-Eye to bring the pickup as close as he could to where Chance still lay unconscious. Then they all joined in carefully lifting him to the truck bed.

"He's going to be all right now," Josie assured Pru with a hug. "You saved his life. You and Bart and Will."

Pru nodded and clasped Josie's hand in relief. "I've got to go with him."

As she climbed up onto the back of the truck, Bart said, "Kleef and Josie—you see to the injured cattle as best you can." He grabbed a rifle from the rack and threw it at the new hand.

Kleef caught it, nodding. "I'll do what needs to be done."

As Pru hunkered down next to Chance, she heard a calf bawling in pain and had to take a deep breath.

"And be careful of that tape," Bart said, over the sound of Moon-Eye putting the pickup in gear. "See if you can figure out a way to disarm it. I sure as hell want to know what happened there."

They started off, Pru checking Chance's vitals.

What *had* happened?

Even though she herself had never lived on a ranch, she knew electric fence tape pulsed—giving out short-lived shocks strong enough to be unpleasant but not enough to kill anything or anyone.

Not unless someone had rigged it with intent.

She didn't have time to follow that line of thought before a groan issued from her patient.

"Chance," she called softly.

His eyes fluttered open to reveal eyes that were dull and filled with confusion. "What…what the hell happened?"

"You died on us, Chance Quarrels, but Bart and I brought you back."

FOR THE LIFE OF HIM Chance couldn't remember what happened, certainly not getting electrocuted. He barely remembered the stampede preceding the incident.

For the life of him…*his life*…lost and then restored by Pru and Bart.

He could hardly fathom it.

But, stuck as he was in an ICU bed at a Taos hospital, hooked up to a cardiac monitor, an IV solution dripping into his arm, he had to believe it.

But how had it happened?

*And why?*

Had the Cowboy Poet somehow tried to make good on his threat to kill him? Only thing…how could anyone be sure that he would step on the live wire…or be sure that someone else wouldn't?

Despite his suspicions, knowing he should stay alert if only to protect himself, should the cause arise,

Chance felt himself drifting off. The stress to his body was too great for him to fight the healing sleep.

Every so often he drifted back to consciousness, almost always because someone had entered his room and was watching over him.

Focusing was an effort, however. Impressions stayed with him, more than anything that was said. Later he sorted through them, like pages in an album.

An unnaturally quiet Pru slipping in and out, leaving him with the memory of her dewy morning scent. Pa, looking like death warmed over, looming nearby for a while. Felice fighting like a cougar for her cub to be allowed to see him when some hospital broomstick got hung up on that "immediate relative" thing.

These visits he remembered, and one other, as well. One not so clear and sharp in his mind.

A dark figure blending with the shadows...a hand reaching toward him through a shaft of light... something sparkling. A ring, he thought.

Fact or fiction? Reality or dream? Chance couldn't say for certain.

Perhaps it had been one of the medical personnel in to check on him. Only he couldn't convince himself of that.

There had been something furtive—threatening?— about this visit. He couldn't get it out of his mind.

The mugging came back to him. The split lip. The certainty that one of his attackers had been wearing a ring. One that sparkled with diamonds? A woman's ring?

Deep in thought, he nearly jumped out of his skin at the sound of footsteps. He whipped his head around toward the door just as Bart entered.

"How are you doing?" Bart asked, keeping his distance, his fingers worrying the brim of his black Stetson.

"Not feelin' like dancin', that's for sure."

His foot pained him where the shock had entered, but his shoulder felt like an open wound, which he knew it was. The electrical current had left a hole in his flesh where it had exited his body.

"You gave us a good scare."

"*Were* you scared, Bart?"

His older brother indulged himself in a long, silent stare before saying, "Don't make me sorry for saving your hide."

Chance cursed himself for the bitter words that always seemed to come so easily when he was around family.

"I'm the one who's sorry," Chance said, his apology sincere. "Reflex, I guess."

"Yeah, a lot of that going around."

Bart's form of apology, Chance guessed, willing to take whatever peace offering his brother was willing to give.

"Before we get into it, I want to thank you for saving my hide, Bart. I'm not ready to go into the next life yet."

"I had the CPR training," Bart said, as if trying to minimize the importance of his fast action. "You would have done the same for me." He arched a dark eyebrow. "You would have, right?"

Chance tried on a grin. "I guess."

But Bart didn't smile in return. Something was obviously whittling away at him inside.

Sobering, Chance asked, "So what's the bad news?"

Bart sat in the chair at the bedside. "Kleef took a ride and found the problem. Power lines were down where they crossed the electric fence…"

"So the tape didn't pulse like it was supposed to, and the high voltage almost killed me," Chance said. "How did the power line come down?"

"Don't know yet. Odd, isn't it?" Bart mused. "Another piece of bad luck following on the heels of Frank's being hurt the other day."

"Mmm."

Chance chose to remain noncommittal on that one. Bad luck, yes, but for him this time, which meant it might not have anything to do with luck at all.

No doubt the lawman in Bart was riled and champing at the bit to investigate. He would be looking hard at that power line area. And, knowing his brother, Chance figured he'd find whatever there was to be found.

That being a given, Chance wondered if he shouldn't break down and tell Bart what had been going on with him and why, before this went any further.

It made all the sense in the world. Pru had thought so when she'd tried to get him to go to Bart after the beating. Bart had helped save his life, making Chance feel a little softer toward his brother, at least for the moment. And Chance was realizing exactly how much danger he was in.

Not to mention the people around him.

If that downed wire had been meant for him, the danger was more immediate than he'd considered. And too often, danger didn't distinguish between its victims.

What if something happened to Pru or anyone else because he was too damn stubborn to be sensible?

He'd just about talked himself into consulting with his brother when Bart said, "So what the hell happened to cause that stampede?"

Chance shook his head. "I couldn't say."

"But you were out there alone."

"Everything about this morning is pretty vague in my head right now." And then it hit him. "You aren't suggesting it was *my* fault?"

"Well, the cows were settled until you had that argument with Pru and rode Predator hard through the herd."

Words that closed Chance off from further good will.

Wondering why he hadn't seen it coming, he wearily said, "Yeah, why not? The stampede was my fault, too. Damn hard work. I'm beat. If you don't mind, I need to be alone to get my rest."

"Chance, I didn't…"

Chance closed his eyes, and Bart let it drop.

The brotherly peace treaty ended before it had even begun.

PRU GOT BACK to the hospital after dark. Justine had been great, staying home from the store all day to take care of the girls. Thankfully, Pru wasn't scheduled into the café for several days, because she intended to remain at Chance's bedside as much as possible until he was released.

But she'd also wanted to bring Hope with her for a short visit—though tempting fate, she just couldn't help herself. Or maybe she'd changed her mind and *did* want Chance to know his daughter. She wasn't willing to analyze her own actions or feelings too closely just yet.

Normally a small child wouldn't be allowed into an ICU, but Pru had lucked out there. She recognized one of the nurses from school—they'd had several classes together. Lauren had given her an okay on bringing the little girl, with the stipulation that Pru needed to keep Hope quiet.

Lauren had also assured Pru that it looked like Chance was going to be as right as rain.

Because his heart had stopped, he'd have to be monitored for at least forty-eight hours, but so far the rhythm was normal. His urine had been checked for by-products of muscle damage, and apparently the effect had been minimal. And while the entry and exit site wounds would have to be cared for beyond his stay, they, too, would heal with time.

So, in a fairly positive mood, Pru sneaked Hope into his room and ignored the medical paraphernalia. Instead, she zeroed in on Chance's sleeping face. Her heart went out to him. His lip might look a bit better, but the discoloration under his eye was blooming.

Overtired and vying for attention, Hope began squirming and jabbering at her.

"Honey, shh." Pru adjusted the toddler's blanket and put a finger to her lips. "We have to be very quiet."

"Why?"

"Because we have a badly injured man here," Pru whispered. "But he's going to be just fine, so don't be scared."

She glanced back at Chance and realized he wasn't asleep at all. He was staring at them, his expression strange. Pru's heart thudded.

*This was it—the moment he would realize that Hope was his daughter.*

But all he said was, "Hey, Squirt, what are you doing here?"

Hope smiled at him, then in an unusual attack of shyness, stuck her thumb in her mouth and buried her face in Pru's shoulder.

Now disappointed that Chance still didn't make the connection, Pru said, "The doctors say you'll live."

"Thanks to you."

"And Bart and Will."

"And them."

"I was so scared, Chance." Hugging Hope to her, she moved closer to the bed. "I've never been scared like that before in my life. If anything had happened to you…what am I saying? Something unthinkable *did* happen—"

"I get your drift."

"About the fight this morning," Pru said, "I'm sorry. I didn't mean to jump to anything. I'm on your side, Chance, I swear. I know you're a good man and that you would never purposely hurt anyone." She was blathering, and he was staring at her with a curious expression. "It's just…I was so worried."

"I don't mean for you to worry about me, Pru." Chance dropped his gaze from hers. "Maybe it was unfair of me, but I was determined to keep you out of it."

"Out of what?"

"The whole robbery thing. You asked me why I came back now?" His eyes met hers. "Well, that was part of the reason."

Heart thumping, Pru lowered herself into the chair. "Because you really are involved?"

"Yeah, I'm involved." His voice filled with what sounded like self-loathing, Chance told her, "I didn't rob or kill anyone, you understand, but the whole bank robbery thing was my ridiculous notion."

Though she was shaking inside, Pru didn't say a word. Clinging to their daughter who seemed to have fallen asleep, she sat staring at Chance. Waiting for the rest.

"I had an off couple of weeks at the rodeos," he began. "I couldn't win an event to save my life. I was distracted. Thinking about other things."

From the way he looked at her, Pru gathered *she* was among those other things.

"Anyway, I was feeling down and disgusted with myself and had a few too many beers with the boys that night."

He stopped then, and Pru feared he might not go on. Softly rubbing Hope's back, she felt the little girl snuggle closer in her sleep. She pressed her cheek against Hope's soft hair. Wondering if she needed to encourage Chance to continue, she hesitated. Perhaps he was merely gathering his thoughts. Or his courage.

"I'd been on a losing streak, but I wasn't close to being broke," he finally went on. "Unfortunately, Lyle Tunney and Hector Moreno were. As day workers, they weren't getting any work, and as rodeo bums, they weren't even making back their entry fees. They were sleeping in their car, bumming food and beers from other cowboys."

"So they were getting desperate for money," she

murmured. Not that it was an excuse for doing anything illegal.

"Tunney was saying something about having to
go live in a city and get real jobs. Moreno vowed
he'd rather die first and said there had to be some
way to stay afloat until their luck changed. He started
speculating about working a shill game with the rodeo audience. Then Tunney said maybe *he* could
learn to pick pockets. We were laughing about the
ridiculousness of it all…and then I had to open my
big mouth."

"You actually told them to rob a bank?"

"It was in jest, Pru. A put on. At least that's the
way I meant it. I suggested they get some six-
shooters and cover their faces with bandannas, then
stage an old-fashioned bank robbery on horseback—
the kind you see in a low-budget Western. We all
laughed about how well that would solve their problems. Moreno brought up the Stockman's Bank of
Trinity in particular. And Tunney got into it, worrying about the getaway on horseback and how a car
might be more practical. Not theirs, of course—it being too old and decrepit. When we went home for
the night, I thought it was forgotten."

"That was it?" Pru breathed a sigh of relief. "If
that was your whole involvement, then—"

"It was enough," Chance interrupted. "Christ,
who would have known they would really do it,
though? I sure didn't, until I caught the news about
the robbery and the security guard's death. And when
I saw the picture from the security cameras, it left
no doubt in my mind."

A joke turned deadly serious, Pru thought. "What
then, Chance?"

"Then I went to the authorities and told them my story."

"They believed you?"

He nodded. "They arrested Moreno and Tunney, but they couldn't find any evidence of the holdup on them or in their car. And while the authorities have the footage from the bank security camera, it's not conclusive because so much of their faces are covered up. The prosecution needs my testimony. Without it, there's no case."

Now it was all starting to make sense, Pru thought. "Moreno and Tunney don't want you to testify. Of course…that's what that Cowboy Code business was all about." But why wasn't Chance doing something about the threats, rather than hiding out? "Can't you just go to the authorities and tell them these men are after you?" she asked. "Surely the prosecutor can provide you with protection. Or at the very least, put Moreno and Tunney back in jail where they belong."

"They are in jail, Pru. No bail money. They were broke, remember? If they bailed themselves out, it would give the prosecution more to work with."

"But if they're not after you, then, who—"

"Good question. Compadres…cousins…hired hands willing to do what it takes to scare me off from testifying? Could be anyone."

*Anyone?*

Fear coursed through Pru, and she started to wonder about the accident that had landed Chance in this hospital bed.

"That's all it is, right, Chance? Scare tactics?" When he didn't immediately agree, she said, "Please tell me what happened today was a freak accident."

"I don't know, Prunella, I surely don't."

Once more Pru felt as if she couldn't breathe. Chance was in danger, she knew it. And there was a very obvious solution to the problem—one she knew he would hate.

"You need to tell Bart what you just told me," she said anyway. "He'll know what to do."

"I'm not involving Bart!" Chance snapped. "And I don't want you to, either."

Fear turned to anger. "Why are you being so pigheaded?" She narrowed her gaze at him. "All of you Quarrels men are alike in that respect."

"I'm nothing like Pa or Bart." Chance's voice rose a notch. "Trust me, they never stop reminding me of that fact."

"It's time you got that chip off your shoulder. Chip...excuse me...it's a whole wooden block!"

Her raised voice woke Hope, who immediately began to fuss.

"Shh, sweetheart, go back to sleep."

But Hope wasn't about to be hushed, and Pru realized she would soon bring a nurse running. Time to leave, at least until she could think about this and figure out a way of talking Chance into being sensible, without losing her temper. Getting to her feet and adjusting her daughter onto her hip, she was thankful that at least the stubborn man would be safe for another day or two in the hospital.

"I have to get Hope home," she told him. "But you think about what I said. And consider whether or not someone just tried to kill you to shut you up. If that's so, then whoever is helping Tunney and Moreno won't quit until they get what they want." She took a deep breath. "And neither will I! Be ready for me, Chance Quarrels,'' she said fiercely, ''because I *will* be back.''

With that, Pru turned from Chance and, feeling his silent gaze boring into her back, left his room.

Hope was crying in earnest now, and Pru tried to soothe her any way she could. ''Here's your blanky, honey,'' she murmured, stuffing the rag-like blanket closer to Hope's face, then kissing her head.

Instinct told Pru to defy Chance and talk to Bart herself, but the idea of losing his trust stopped her. He had finally given her the truth. She didn't want him to regret that.

She left the hospital, and as she crossed the parking lot, she tried to think of a way to convince Chance that he needed his brother's help before it was too late. Unfortunately she couldn't find the ace in the hole she needed.

Once she arrived at her vehicle, Pru balanced a still-sniffling Hope on one hip and slipped a hand into her jeans pocket. No car keys.

''Double damnation!'' she muttered, switching the toddler to the other hip.

Intent on finding the keys in one of her other pockets, Pru was unaware of another presence until she was successful and about to unlock the door. That's when she caught the reflection in the window—a man with a hat brim pulled low, face covered by a bandanna.

Her heart nearly stopped…

Knowing it was too late to run, she opened her mouth to scream even as a cloth with a familiar cloying smell was pressed to her face.

Her thoughts muddled before drifting off altogether….

## Chapter Nine

Hope's indignant screams cut through Pru's unconscious, and she felt as if she were struggling up from the depths of hell to get to her daughter.

From somewhere nearby she heard "I don't know how to make no kid stop cryin' any more than you do."

"You're a woman—this is supposed to come natural to you!"

Hog-tied, Pru lay on her side on a narrow cot and focused on the voices to clear her mind. Moonlight filtering through a filthy window cast a bluish glow on a narrow room, nearly barren but for the cot and a single wooden chair. A rim of faint golden light from an adjoining room set the location of the door for her.

"M'ma!"

Her daughter's frantic scream ripping right through her, Pru croaked, "Hope, honey, it's okay sweetheart! Mama's here!" Her throat felt dry and raw, but at least they hadn't gagged her.

"You hear something?" came the man's voice.

"She's awake."

"Hey, get the kid to stop cryin'!" he yelled over Hope's continuing wail.

Pru yelled back, "How do you propose I do that when I can't even touch her?"

*"M'ma!"*

"Get in there and untie her," the woman said.

"But we're not—"

"Don't argue. Do you wanna listen to that kid squall all night?"

"All right!"

The door swung open and Pru squinched her eyes against the sudden and painful light. Her heart thumped with fear, more for Hope than for herself. A large silhouette loomed over her, and a moment later her hands and feet were freed. Before she could rub the circulation back into her wrists, Hope was shoved into her arms by a slightly shorter if equally solid figure—the woman of the pair.

Wrapping her arms around her daughter and kissing her little face, Pru said, "Everything is going to be all right now, sweetheart," even though she didn't believe a word of it.

Hope clung to her and sobbed desperately. Pru rocked her child and stroked her back. Tears shuddered at the back of Pru's eyelids, but her crying wouldn't get them anywhere. She stared up at the combined silhouettes blocking most of the light from the doorway. No matter how she tried she couldn't make out anything more distinctive than their profiles.

"Why isn't that kid quieting down?" the man demanded.

"You've frightened her," Pru said, holding on to

her temper. She had to play this smart. "I hope you had the sense to bring the bag along."

"What bag?" This from the man.

Though Hope was calming down now that she was in her mother's arms, she didn't stop crying, which Pru decided was to their advantage.

"The one with her diapers and formula," she told them. "Poor baby's wet. And all that crying has probably made her hungry, too." She thought fast, already formulating a plan. "So if you *didn't* bring the diaper bag, you might as well let us go now, because she can keep this up longer than you can stand it. Trust me."

Though she doubted they'd let her walk, she figured one of them would have to find a store in the middle of the night—which would probably be the man—and she might have a chance at escape.

A prospect that was dashed when the woman said, "I can't stand it now—get the bag or we won't be getting any sleep tonight."

Pru heard keys being exchanged and figured they'd brought her station wagon.

"Yeah, you be careful," the man muttered, backing off.

And the woman warned her, "Don't try nothin' if you know what's good for you."

"What do you want with us?" Pru asked, hoping against hope that she'd been mistaken for someone else. "Why have you brought us here?"

"Save the questions, honey. Tend to your kid before I go nuts."

Pru hugged Hope to her but didn't work at shushing her. Obviously her cries were throwing their kidnappers off balance. Maybe her talking would, too.

"If it's about money, I promise you I don't have any." Pru made her words run together annoyingly. "I work as a waitress for heaven's sake—"

The woman's "Shut your yap" encouraged Pru to keep it up.

"But you can have my station wagon—just take it—I won't even report it missing."

"Forget it. It's not about money. Hell, it's not about you."

Pru's heart fell. Though expected, they were words she hadn't wanted to hear.

*Chance…*

Playing dumb, she asked, "Then what is it about?"

The man's return stopped any reply from the woman.

"Here you go," he growled, throwing the diaper bag down on the cot next to Pru.

Frustrated and concerned for her daughter, Pru concentrated on changing Hope's diaper in the near dark. She was still a little woozy—whether from the drug or fright, she wasn't certain.

What she did know without being told was that this was about Chance and that damn Cowboy Code. But while one of the kidnappers must be the cowboy poet—and must have seen her visiting Chance and made assumptions about their relationship—that didn't tell her how *they* were involved in this operation.

Whatever their connection, Pru now feared they had the leverage needed to get Chance to recant.

CHANCE WOKE TO FIND streaks of dawn barely lighting the horizon and a weather front moving in.

He was well rested and feeling as fit as he ever had. His first clear thoughts were of Pru and the way she'd handled the truth when he'd finally given it to her.

Pru hadn't seemed overly shocked. Distressed, yes, but that was to be expected. More important, she hadn't placed blame. Or she hadn't said the words. When he'd refused to go to Bart, she'd been angry enough to leave, though, and he figured getting Hope home had been an excuse.

*Why had she brought the little girl in the first place?*

Not wanting to think too closely on it, Chance was glad to put the puzzle aside when a young aide entered with his breakfast tray.

He mustered up a smile. "My gruel?"

The young woman wrinkled her nose. "Sorry about that. But it looks like you got a card to cheer you up. That should make the gruel taste better, right?"

"It's bound to," Chance agreed as she set the tray in front of him.

"Need help?"

"Thanks, darlin', but I think I can handle it."

Smiling, the young woman left.

Thinking the card was from Pru—her way of making up with him, perhaps?—Chance eagerly fetched it from his tray. But once he saw his name printed across the envelope, the breath caught in his throat.

The printing was familiar…

He opened the envelope fast, slipped out the piece of paper and unfolded it.

Denying the Cowboy Code
by the Cowboy Poet

Denying the Cowboy Code isn't smart,
especially in matters of the heart.
One last chance to make it right,
or plan to sleep alone tonight.

Chance's mouth went dry as he realized the bastard was threatening him with Pru's safety.

He had to warn her. Tell her to make sure she glued herself to her sister or brother-in-law until he got out of here. Then he could get her someplace safe. He hoped. He grabbed the telephone and dialed the Garner number, praying Pru herself would pick up.

"Hello?" The feminine and sleepy voice was her sister's.

"Justine, it's Chance. I need to speak to Pru. Right now."

Obviously his urgency transmitted to her, for she didn't question him, merely said, "Hang on a minute," and set down the receiver.

Knots tied up his gut as he waited. He took several deep breaths and started to relax, until he heard the receiver being picked up again.

"She's not here, Chance," Justine said, sounding concerned. "She must still be at the hospital."

"No, she left last night, said she had to get Hope home."

"Hope's not in her crib, either—I checked. What about the waiting room?"

"I didn't think of that."

He signed off quickly, telling Justine he would have Pru call as soon as he located her...registering the fact that, while Justine had sounded worried, she hadn't been anywhere near hysterical about little Hope being gone.

Encumbered by the cardiac monitor hookup and the IV still dripping solution into his arm, Chance wasn't going anywhere himself. He hit the buzzer attached to his bed.

"Nurses' station," came the scratchy voice over the monitor.

"Could someone check the waiting room for a woman with a little girl?"

"Sure, I can take a peek. What's her name?"

"Prudence Prescott."

Chance couldn't ease back and wait. Every second that ticked by seemed like a minute. Minutes he was wasting when he knew in his gut that Pru and Hope were nowhere around.

He began peeling away one of the electrodes when the voice came back over the monitor. "Mr. Quarrels, I'm sorry, but there's no one in the waiting room at all."

Exactly what he'd feared.

He had to get out of there…had to find Pru…had to make sure that she and Squirt were all right. He ripped the electrode tape free, tightening his jaw when chest hair came with it.

"Mr. Quarrels?" came the concerned voice at the other end of the monitor.

But Chance was concentrating on the tangle of wires that held him prisoner. He'd pulled two more electrodes free before a nurse rushed into his room.

"What do you think you're doing?"

"Leaving."

"The doctor didn't clear you. He probably won't until tomorrow morning at the earliest."

"I'm clearing myself," Chance told her, continuing to free himself. "You can't keep me here if I don't want to stay."

He turned his attention to the IV secured to the back of his hand.

"Stop that." She held his free hand before he could get to the tape. "You do realize you had a very serious electrical injury that stopped your heart, right?"

"So I've been told."

"If you leave we can't be responsible—"

"I'll check my damn self out! I'll sign papers. Whatever you require. But I have to get out of here *now!*"

His pulse seemed to flutter for a second, and Chance knew he had to keep calm or he wouldn't be able to help anyone, let alone himself.

Only…how could he keep calm when the woman he loved and her child were missing?

How was she going to get them away from their kidnappers?

That thought had played over and over in Pru's head throughout the night. Now the sky was streaked with rays of light, and still she had no answers.

Before they'd left her alone with her daughter, she'd plied her captors with nonstop questions until the woman had threatened to tape her mouth shut. So much for talking her way out of the situation. All she'd gotten for her effort was the certainty that the two weren't a couple, didn't even seem to like each other.

Once left alone, she'd attempted to open the window, but, to her frustration, it had been nailed shut. Then, hours ago, she'd cracked the door in hopes of sneaking out, but she'd heard one of them moving around.

Everything seemed quiet now, except for an occasional neigh from one of the horses out in the lean-to.

What in the world did they need horses for?

Putting the animals to the back of her mind, Pru decided at another escape attempt.

As far as she could tell, they were in the middle of nowhere. High desert country. The building that housed them had probably been some early rancher's home—main room, two bedrooms and a bathroom with barely usable plumbing. Now the place was nothing more than a dusty hovel with a few pieces of worn furniture.

If she made it, Pru had no idea of where she'd be headed. The sun was rising in the east but so was the weather. She could smell rain coming. And she had no clue of where they were in relation to a town or anything else. Still, she had to try to escape, if not for herself, for her daughter.

Luckily she always kept a spare set of keys to her station wagon in the diaper bag.

Hope was sleeping, but when Pru picked up the toddler, she stirred and mewled a protest. ''Shh, go back to sleep, sweetheart. Dream good dreams.''

Waiting until the little body went limp against her, Pru moved to the door and carefully inched it open, cringing when the hinges creaked.

She waited. When no shout of alarm went up, she peeked through the crack to make sure she saw no one. She already had her bearings—she'd been allowed to go to the bathroom earlier, escorted by the woman who'd stood in the doorway on guard. While a few strands of blond hair had escaped her hat, her features had been covered by a bandanna.

Just as well. She didn't want to know what either of them looked like. If she did...well, she didn't want to think about what would happen then.

The door opposite, which led to the outside, was Pru's goal. As far as she could tell from her limited viewpoint, all was clear. That didn't make her heart pound any slower or her mouth any less dry.

With Hope pressed to her securely, Pru crept through the opening, then moved with stealth toward the outside door that promised freedom from their captors. She'd gotten halfway across the room and was experiencing a kind of euphoria when the man's voice burst her balloon and brought her sailing back down to reality.

"And where do you think you're goin'?"

*Double damnation!*

Ready to jump out of her skin, Pru froze, then got hold of herself. She turned and spotted him deep in shadow. "Uh, I was just needing the bathroom."

"With your kid?"

"I thought you didn't want her to cry." She shook Hope's leg furtively so her daughter half woke and did exactly that. "Oh, darn, there she goes again. It's all right, sweetheart, you don't have to cry. Mama's here."

A little soothing back rub and Hope quieted once more. And Pru turned, as if meaning to complete her journey to the bathroom.

"You're headed for the wrong door."

"Am I?" she asked with fake innocence. She thought it worth a try. "Oh. I guess I'm not awake yet." Wearing an innocent expression that belied her hair-trigger tension, she faced him. "Which one?"

A silence hung between them as if he were sizing her up. A trickle of sweat wended its way down Pru's spine. It took all her acting skills to keep from looking guilty.

Finally he pointed. "There. And don't be long."

"Right."

She felt his eyes follow her across the room. Once inside the bathroom she shook with relief, but she didn't have time to indulge herself. She checked the window, something she hadn't been able to do with her female captor standing over her. It, like the bedroom window, had been nailed shut.

*What now?*

As she used the facility to calm her nerves and the man's suspicion, her mind whirled and formulated an alternative plan. The woman of the pair was a hard one and seemed to be in charge. But for the moment, at least, she was out of the way, and Pru could concentrate on her partner.

*But how?*

Distract him and when his back was turned, whack him over the head?

Not her forte.

Pru had to admit she was better at talking her way out of bad situations than she was at dealing with violence. But she'd never had so much at stake before. Somehow she would have to try to gain the man's sympathy.

Gathering her courage and praying that she would get this one right, Pru left the bathroom. Two steps past the doorway, and she almost ran straight into their captor. His hat was pulled down over his forehead and the bandanna again covered the lower half of his face. His shadowed eyes were dead on her.

Unnerved once more, she nevertheless asked, "Do you mind if we stay out here for a few minutes?" She shuddered convincingly. "I have a thing about small places."

"Just don't try nothin'."

Pru laid Hope down on the couch and, keeping a soothing hand on her tummy, sat next to her. Their captor moved to the chair opposite, where he'd been earlier, but he remained standing. Staring.

Pru calmed herself inside. She could do this. She could do anything she had to in order to keep Hope safe. Even pull off a miracle.

"Can't you tell me what this is all about?" she asked. "Please? I'll cooperate with you. I don't want anything to happen to my little girl."

"Nothing's going to happen to either of you if your man does the right thing."

"Man?" She pretended obliviousness. "I...I don't have a husband."

"Boyfriend, then."

"Not one of those, either." Giving him a disgusted frown, she said, "In case you didn't know, men aren't much interested in single mothers." Or so she'd been told since she hadn't been looking.

"What do you call Chance Quarrels?"

*There it was, then!*

Pru took a big breath, screwed her face into a mask of fury and flew to her feet, saying, "I call Chance Quarrels a two-timing, good-for-nothing, lowlife, back-stabbing, miserly snake!"

And prayed she wouldn't burn in hell for telling such an awful lie.

"Huh?" The man narrowed his gaze above the bandanna. "I don't believe you."

"Believe me."

"You've been seen with him. And when we picked you up, you were at the hospital, visiting him."

"I've been trying to get him to do the right thing. I was at the hospital to give him one last chance." She stepped closer so he could look into her lying eyes and hopefully read tragedy there. "Bad enough he ran out on *me* in my hour of need." Pinching herself hard where he couldn't see, she prompted her eyes to shine with unshed tears. "But now he refuses to support his own daughter."

"The kid is *his?*"

Too late Pru realized her mistake. Of course he hadn't known. How could he, when Chance didn't even know?

"Damn shame when a man won't take care of his own," the man muttered.

Pru quickly jumped on the unexpected opening.

"And after all we shared. He took my innocence and then ran off with another woman—" she forced her voice to tremble "—so of course he believes the worst of me. He refuses to believe Hope is his."

"The bastard!"

"I'm doing the best I can for our daughter, but waitressing three nights a week—well, that's just the bare necessities." That part certainly was true. "If my sister hadn't taken me in, I don't know what we'd do. Why, we'd be homeless."

"You poor thing. My mama had a rough time, too. There were three of us kids…"

Pru couldn't believe her good fortune. Her blatant lies were getting to the bad guy!

"And now you think you'll force Chance to do something for you because you're holding us hostage." Pru shook her head and allowed a few tears to roll down her cheeks. "But he won't, because he doesn't care a thing about us. Oh, Hope, baby, we're doomed."

The man reached out and patted her shoulder. "No, nothing bad—"

"What a load of bull!" came the strident female voice that made Pru shudder for real. "Just take your hands off her before she gets the jump on you."

"Now wait here—"

"And don't believe a word out of her mouth…except maybe for the part about the kid belonging to Quarrels."

The woman snorted behind her bandanna, and from her waistband freed a six-shooter that looked decidedly clumsy in a hand decorated with long, polished nails and a fancy ring. Pru could also see mascara-laden brown eyes narrowed speculatively at her.

"Now that's a bonus I didn't expect," the woman mused. "With the brat as bait, we have no reason to keep the preacher's daughter around at all…."

SLEEP DEPRIVED, guilt crawling along his nerves, Emmett strode through the front entrance of the hospital just as Chance came down the hall wearing the change of clothes Felice had brought him.

"What in tarnation—"

"Pa, what are you doing here so early?"

Chance cut him off before Emmett could find out why his boy was out of his hospital bed.

"I never went home," Emmett said. "I needed to make certain you were all right."

"You've been here all night?"

"In your room...out in the waiting room...here outside."

He'd been there to register all the visitors who'd come to check on his son, from the two women who loved him to the ranch hands—Moon-Eye, Will and Kleef—and even a few people he hadn't recognized, among them an attractive woman and a big guy with whitish hair.

Not that they'd all been allowed in Chance's room. But at least they'd shown their concern by stopping by to inquire after his son.

"Pa, you need sleep."

"It wasn't like I didn't try. But I couldn't get more than a couple of winks at a time. Been wandering around talking to myself like a crazy person. Can't imagine why no one has locked me up."

"Well, it's a good thing you're here. You can drive me to the Curly-Q."

Emmett was taken aback. "I thought you were supposed to stay for a couple of days' observation."

Chance remained evasive, saying only, "Yeah, I thought so, too. But I'm fine, so can we get out of here?"

Rather than question him, which would only have aggravated them both, Emmett led the way to the ranch truck. He considered the overcast sky, decided they could beat the rain home.

How had the boy meant to get anywhere in his condition? Rent a car? Hitchhike?

And why the hurry?

He kept an eye on Chance as his son climbed into the passenger seat and settled back. The boy seemed okay, so Emmett got behind the wheel and cranked the engine to life.

"Staying up all night and worrying can't be good for your heart, Pa."

"Damn my heart!" Emmett nearly shouted. "It's you I'm concerned about right now. You could have died...and it would have been my fault."

"Why? Because you asked me to come home?"

*Home...*

Chance normally avoided the word like the plague but there it was, Emmett thought. The Curly-Q was his home, no matter how torn he felt about the idea.

Guilt shot through Emmett anew. The boy wouldn't have come home if it wasn't for him. For his scheming. He was to blame.

As if Chance could read his mind, he said, "It wasn't your fault, Pa. *You* didn't bring down that power line. Are you going to tell me that you know who did?"

Emmett shook his head. "I only wish."

"Then let it go. Take a deep breath and let it go."

"I can't. I got to fix things." He should have taken care of it when it started. "I don't know how, but I'll figure it out."

"Pa, please relax, would you," Chance said in his most congenial tone, as if he was trying to defuse the head of steam his father was working up. "And when we get home, you get some sleep before you have another heart attack. Then it'll be me visiting you in an I.C.U., and trust me, if I never see one of those rooms again, it'll be too soon."

Somehow Emmett pulled himself together and started the truck. "Yeah, okay. I'll sleep. But I swear to you, Chance, someone is going to be held accountable for what happened to you."

Even now Emmett could hardly believe he'd nearly lost one of his boys over a piece of land.

# Chapter Ten

A foreign emotion filled Chance as he realized how worried his father was about him, how much he must care. Something made him respond in kind. For once in his life he felt a little closer to the parent who'd pushed him away more times than he could remember.

He only wondered how the old man would react when he finally learned the truth.

*The truth...*

Who had been telling it?

Certainly he wasn't the only guilty one in that respect. Remembering Bart had been stewing about all the bad luck the ranch had been having, Chance figured there was something the old man hadn't told them. But that could wait. He had more important things on his mind.

Pru and Hope being number one.

He checked the parking lot quickly as they drove through. No sign of a beat-up station wagon. Not that he'd expected to set eyes on it. Not after the latest threat from the Cowboy Poet. Not after checking with personnel before leaving the hospital.

The night receptionist just going off shift had re-

membered seeing Pru and Hope go out the night before. But no one he could find had actually seen
whether or not they'd been alone getting into the
station wagon. Likewise, no one had seen her vehicle
pulling out of the lot.

Yeah, someone would pay, Chance thought as his
father drove in silence—especially if anything bad
had happened to Pru or her little girl.

He'd call Justine again as soon as they got back
to the ranch. If she hadn't heard from Pru by then,
he had only one resort open to him. Bart. No excuses
this time. He would tell his brother the truth—the
whole truth—and enlist his aid in tracking down the
woman he loved and her child.

*Her child...*

Why hadn't he seen it from the first?

He'd just assumed Hope was another of Justine's
kids. The conclusion had been logical. The three little
girls looked like matching stepping stones, even as
Justine and Pru had looked so much alike while
growing up.

But Hope's room being right next to Pru's...the
intimate bond she obviously had with the child...
he'd been staring at the truth all along and not seeing
it.

So why hadn't she told him?

He guessed they hadn't done much talking in the
three days he'd been back, at least not about anything
other than the trouble he was in. But now it made
sense—her not welcoming him with open arms.
Well, she might not have done that, anyway, what
with his being gone so long and all. He'd left her
hanging, and she'd obviously turned to someone else

for comfort, and a bright, happy daughter had been the result.

He didn't want to think about Pru with another man—the very idea tore up his gut. But he couldn't blame her. That he would put on his own, albeit overcrowded, shoulders. If she'd turned to another, it was because he hadn't been there. He'd told her he loved her and then he'd left her as always.

Maybe she'd been looking for someone more permanent. Obviously she'd gotten another dose of the same.

Pru must have felt so abandoned yet again. And what about Hope?

Perhaps she was too young to understand now, but in a few years she would start to wonder what was wrong with her, what she had done to drive away her own father. Having lived with the consequences of having been abandoned by his mother when he wasn't much older than Hope, Chance wondered what kind of bastard would run out on his own child.

He'd barely met Pru's little girl and already he had warm feelings for her. She was so innocent—he'd give anything to be able to protect her, not only from the clutches of the Cowboy Poet, but from all of life's disappointments.

Maybe, if they all came out of this in one piece, Pru would give him that honor.

"You okay?"

Pa's sudden question startled Chance out of his reverie. "What? Yeah, fine." He looked around and realized they were nearing Silver Springs. "Just thinking."

"Been doing a heap of that lately myself, Son."

"About the ranch?"

"About everything. Especially about my boys. About how I never properly appreciated you all, how maybe I never made you feel as special as I oughta've. It shouldn't take bad times to bring a family together."

Chance figured this was as close to an admission of guilt and love as he would ever hear from his father. Truthfully it surprised and touched him.

"We can work on it, Pa, if that's what you want."

"You won't get yourself in a fit to wander off to God knows where?"

"I didn't say I wouldn't ever leave the Curly-Q again." Although whether or not he would and for how long now was up in the air. If he had to recant his testimony to save Pru and Hope, he would do so, even if it landed him in a jail cell. "But I'll always come back…if that's okay with you."

"Don't talk nonsense. Of course you can. The Curly-Q is your home, boy. I'd rather you stuck around full-time…but if you can't…well, coming back whenever you can is okay. Why do you think I had Howard Siles draw up them papers to make the spread and the rest of my holdings into a family corporation?"

Why did you? hovered on Chance's tongue, but he kept himself from challenging the old man.

It was enough that his father had made the offer. At least for now. Chance kept his own counsel the rest of the way to the ranch.

The sky spritzed them for a few minutes, then stopped. Sensing they were in for more than a sprinkle, Chance hoped the fact wouldn't interfere with his plans to find Pru and Hope.

When they arrived, he looked at the place he'd

known all his life with a slightly different appreciation. The sprawling adobe with added-on wings really was his home. The earth-colored walls, brightened by blue trim, were as familiar to him as his own face in a mirror. Rather, what his face normally looked like, he thought ruefully.

They entered only to find that Felice was alone.

"Mr. Bart already took the hands and Daniel out on the range, and Lainey left for school," Felice told him. Then she hugged him gently, as if he were breakable. "Ah, my Chance," she murmured, a tremble in her voice. "Your being here is so good...I am so thankful...but this is too soon. You shouldn't be on your feet."

Chance hugged her back. "I'm fine, Felice. But Pa's the one who's the worse for wear." He looked even more tired than when they'd left the hospital. "See if you can convince him to take a lie-down, would you?"

But, as usual, his father didn't take to suggestion well. "Now wait just a minute!"

"Mr. Emmett—"

"Don't give me any grief, woman."

"I won't if you do as your son suggests."

They began a staring match, and to Chance's surprise, his father abruptly ended the contest.

"All right. I'll go," he grumbled, turning toward his quarters. "But it's not right—a man being ganged up on in his own home. I won't sleep none anyhow."

Felice said, "I'll get you some herbal tea. That will help relax you." Then she turned to Chance. "What about you? You must be hungry."

"Can't say that I am, Felice." How could he eat

when he was so worried? "But I could use a cup of coffee." The caffeine would keep him going.

"After your heart stopped?" Felice shook her head and gave him a look that reminded him of Pru when she got mad. "I won't be responsible. Herbal tea will do *you* good, as well."

The moment Felice left for the kitchen, Chance went to the nearest phone in the living room and called Justine.

"Have you heard from Pru?" he asked, almost as soon as she said hello.

"I was hoping *you* had. Chance, what's going on?" she asked, voice tight. "Exactly how worried should I be?"

"I'm not sure yet," he said, though he was plenty worried. "I'll find them, Justine, I promise you. I won't let anything happen to either of them."

"I'm counting on you, Chance. And Pru will be counting on you, too. Just don't let her down this time."

Hearing another message in there that he didn't have time to figure out, he said, "I won't."

Chance hung up the receiver and realized he would have to do something he dreaded. He'd have to ride out and find Bart and tell him everything. He only prayed that his brother would know how to handle this.

If anything happened to Pru or Hope…

He stopped in the kitchen to tell Felice that he was leaving. The tea was ready, and she forced him not only to drink it, but to have a homemade muffin, as well. For once, Chance had no appreciation for her culinary skills. He didn't even taste the muffin—it merely filled a hole.

"What's going on, Chance?" Felice asked, sitting opposite him. "No more evasions, please. Why aren't you still at the hospital? What are you so worried about?"

Chance couldn't lie to the woman who was the only mother he had ever known. "At the moment, I'm worried about finding Pru and her daughter."

He gave Felice the long story's short version, skipping over his guilt about suggesting the robbery as a joke, merely filling her in on his upcoming testimony, the Cowboy Poet's threats and Pru and Hope's disappearance.

When he came to the last, Felice appeared stricken, her naturally warm-toned skin looking almost gray. *"Dios!"* she whispered.

"Yeah." He rose. "It's time I enlisted Bart's help, Felice. Past time, really. If I had—but there's no use speculating." Still, a growing guilt nagged at him. He'd handled this all wrong. "I'm going to ride out and find him."

"Does your father know?"

"I didn't want to worry him with his bad heart and all. He's got enough on his mind as is."

"I won't lie to him for you."

"I'm hoping that won't be an issue." Not that his father shouldn't know the truth—just, hopefully, after the fact. "I hope we'll find Pru and Hope before explanations are necessary."

He hugged her.

Her dark eyes luminous with threatening tears, Felice gently touched his bruised face. "My prayers go with you and Pru and...the little one."

Chance held her hand and kissed it before he left. He headed straight for the bunkhouse to get his gear. Noting the loose band of horses was nearby, he whistled sharply a few times, certain they would be curious enough to see what he wanted. Slowly they edged closer. He whistled again before entering the bunkhouse.

By the time he hauled out his saddle and a halter and was heading for the corral, a blue roan had picked her way closer and was eyeing him with interest.

"Hey, darlin', want to stretch your legs some?" Chance murmured.

He set the saddle over the corral fence. Then he held out his hand so the mare could snuffle up his scent and get to know him. Touching her velvet nose and graceful neck, Chance felt the roan shudder under his touch. A little edgy. Not that he minded. She'd be a piece of cake compared to his rides at the rodeo.

The rumble of an engine coming from deep in the canyon caught his attention. Good. That meant Moon-Eye had returned and could tell him exactly where to find Bart.

As the vehicle roared closer, Chance talked to the mare, keeping his voice seductive. He ran his hands all over her before introducing the bridle. She took the bit easily and stood still as he saddled her.

He was fastening the cinch when the approaching truck screeched around a bend and took the uneven dirt and rock road so fast that all the vehicle's loose metal parts seemed to whack against one another. Alarmed, the roan whinnied deep in her throat and danced away.

"What the hell?" Chance muttered as he grabbed her reins and got her under control.

Was Moon-Eye drunk or just being stupid?

Chance spun around to look as the vehicle bounced into view. His heart fluttered alarmingly. Not Moon-Eye's truck but Pru's station wagon!

Dropping the reins, he left the roan and jogged toward the oncoming vehicle. Through the red dust on the windshield, he noted the even darker, brighter-red hair.

"Pru!" he yelled, waving his hat at her.

She seemed to be driving blind, as she didn't immediately slow. Chance had to jump off the path before the vehicle finally ground to a halt.

The door flew open and Pru almost fell out of the driver's seat. Going down to her knees, she frantically scrambled back to her feet. She looked awful—hair tangled, face tearstained, eyes too bright, pasty-faced—but she was the most beautiful sight he had ever seen.

Moving toward her with open arms, he said, "Prunella, you're all right! Thank God!"

She shook her head like a crazed woman. "No...no...no!"

"What is it?" he demanded, looking past her to realize the vehicle was empty. "Where's Squirt?"

An incomprehensible wail of words escaped Pru, making Chance's heart beat double time as he wound his arms around her to keep her from falling.


"THEY HAVE HER!" Pru cried, clutching Chance's shirtfront. She felt as if she were about to pass out, but she couldn't allow herself the luxury of such weakness. She had to stay strong if she wanted to get her daughter back. "The kidnappers rode off into the wilderness with Hope!"

"Who? Did you recognize them?"

"A big man and a tall blond woman, but I never saw their faces, except for the woman's eyes, that is—brown with lots of mascara. They wore bandannas," she explained, "just like your attackers. Maybe they were the ones who mugged you."

Chance nodded. "Most likely, since I got another warning from the Cowboy Poet this morning, a special treat that came with breakfast."

He didn't have to say the warning had to do with her. No doubt that's why he'd left his hospital bed at least a day too soon—to make sure that she was safe.

She might be, but...

"They told me I'll never see Hope again unless I convince you to change your mind about testifying!" Not that she wanted Chance to back out when a murder was involved and the man's death was already on his conscience. "They're going to hold her until the trial is called off and Moreno and Tunney are released."

But panic rose in Pru again at the very thought of her daughter's fate in the kidnappers' hands. Hope's screams at being ripped away from the comfort of her mother's arms echoed in Pru's head. They'd haunted every moment of her wild ride to find help and probably would stay with her until her child was safe in her arms once more.

But what was to make the kidnappers keep their promise and free Hope, even if Chance recanted?

"Oh, God...oh, God...oh, God...what are we going to do?"

"I'm going to find her," Chance said, his expression grim. Then he kissed her forehead comfortingly. "I'm here for you, Pru."

"I knew I could count on you, Chance," she murmured, arching her neck to look deep into his eyes. "I knew I could trust you." He drew her in. How could she have doubted him, even for a moment? "I always knew in my heart that you were a good man."

Only a really good man would volunteer to go find a child he didn't even know was his.

That she'd known what Chance was all along was why she'd waited for him. She admitted it now. As angry as she'd been at him, deep inside she'd wanted him to come back to her. *To them.* For a moment she believed in the fantasy of a family—the two of them and their child.

But Chance still thought Hope was Justine's, because she hadn't trusted him with the truth.

"Prunella," he murmured, "if anything had happened to you...my heart would have broken."

As hers had almost been when she'd thought he was going to die.

"But I'm all right, and you are, too...you are, aren't you?" she asked, suddenly worried that he might not be.

"I am now."

He kissed her then. Not a kiss of unbridled passion, but one that went far, far beyond the physical. A kiss filled with love and comfort and thankfulness. She felt his gratitude deep in her very soul.

Then he gripped her upper arms and held her away from him, so she had to look him in the eyes. "And Hope will be all right, too," he promised. "I'm going to bring her home to you."

Startled, Pru shook her head. "You're not going anywhere without me."

"I'll have to take a horse to track the kidnappers. You're in no condition to ride."

She pulled herself free and swiped the back of a hand over her eyes to remove another round of threatening tears. "You're not leaving me behind, Chance Quarrels. If I can't ride, then I'll crawl after you."

Pru wasn't bluffing, and she could tell he knew it.

"All right. We don't have time to argue the point, so let's get you a mount."

Chance whistled and moved toward the tack shed at one end of the corral, where he hauled out a saddle. Pru followed suit and gathered a bridle and blanket.

A few of the loose horses were meandering closer. Setting down the saddle, Chance directed his gaze to a chestnut mare and moved in on her. A moment later he was leading her back to the corral area.

"I'll tack her up for you," he said, running his hand over the mare's back. "Then we'll go find Bart and—"

"No! It's too late for that—it would take too long," Pru insisted. "The rains could come at any time. The kidnappers will get clear away and we'll never find them."

"You have a point. How much of a head start do they have on us?" Chance asked as he bridled the mare.

"Not much. Less than an hour, I think. They were keeping Hope and me at some rundown house at the north end of the property."

"Near the old mine?"

Pru frowned. "I think so. The house had a main room and two bedrooms and inside facilities. Out back, there was a lean-to in a small corral for the horses."

Chance nodded. "I know the place—Reed and I used to play there when we were kids. It's not far from the mine." He set the saddle blanket in place. "Did you see what direction the kidnappers headed?"

"West."

"Uphill," Chance mused. "That could be tough going. We're going to need water." He hefted the saddle into his arms. "You'll find a couple of canteens inside the bunkhouse, on a peg near the door."

"I'll get them."

Pru made her legs move despite the tremendous effort it took. Stress and lack of food had taken its toll on her. That meant trying not to think about Hope too closely or she would lose it again.

At least she herself was alive, Pru thought gratefully, though she'd suspected the blonde would just as soon have shot her dead if she'd had her druthers.

Instead, the man had unhooked her vehicle's battery to give them a few minutes to get away. Pru would have followed them had they not gone up a rocky incline. No way would her old station wagon have managed. So she'd headed for the sun until she'd hit Silverado Creek.

And then the irony of the kidnappers being on Curly-Q land, right under Chance's nose, so to speak, had hit her. Pru wondered how they'd even known about the house, unless one of them was a local.

Not that she had a clue as to either of their identities.

After filling the canteens, Pru raided the fridge, found some cooked sausage, cheese, bread and fruit and tossed all into a cloth bag.

Who knew how long they would be out there?

She grabbed an apple and, leaving the bunkhouse, ate it while she made her way back to Chance. He was talking to Felice, who appeared appropriately alarmed.

Chance hugged the housekeeper and mounted, then led the chestnut to Pru. She didn't miss the rifles in the leather saddle holsters that he must have retrieved from the tack shed—one for each of them. Nor the sheathed knife hanging from his belt. Of course she knew they needed to be armed—the kidnappers were—but it scared her spitless, anyway.

"I told Felice what happened," Chance told her. "She'll get the message to Bart as soon as anyone rides in."

"Good."

Splitting the core and what apple was left into two pieces, Pru gave it to the horses. Then she handed Chance one of the canteens and hooked the other around her saddle horn.

"Food," she said, handing him the bag.

He'd also secured bedrolls to both saddles and a coil of rope and a set of leather bags to his own. He unfastened one of them and secured the food inside.

"Can you mount on your own?" he asked.

Revitalized by the simple piece of fruit, she countered, "Can you trust that I'm probably in better shape than you are for the moment?"

He didn't argue with that.

Mustering her reserve, Pru practically flew atop the chestnut mare. She turned to wave at Felice, who stood staring after them, the rising wind buffeting her. She looked her age today. And strangely vulnerable. Her stricken gaze ambushed Pru, even at a distance.

Making Pru's breath catch in her throat.

Felice had always treated Chance as she would a son, which would make Hope the grandchild Felice would never otherwise have. In that instant of connection between women who had a man they loved as a common bond, Pru was certain Felice knew.

*Felice knew and Chance didn't....*

Thunder rumbling in the distance snapped Pru into action. She moved the chestnut out, saying, "Let's go find Hope before the skies open." And wondering how and when she was going to tell Chance that the little girl he'd volunteered to save was really their daughter.

HOURS PASSED and they were long off Curly-Q property. They'd reached the foothills of the Sangre de Cristo Range and were wending their way through areas of Gambel Oak and Ponderosa Pine wedged between formations of rock.

And still Chance remained as focused on catching up to the kidnappers as when they had started out.

He'd easily picked up the tracks only to lose them for a while when they'd reached an area that was all rock. They'd lost some time then, but he figured carrying a small child who had to be fed and changed wasn't easy going. The kidnappers had been forced to stop more often and longer than he and Pru would. He'd found the signs of that, too.

Chance couldn't imagine what Pru was going through, worrying about Hope. For the moment she was keeping those emotions locked up tight inside herself.

And she still hadn't even admitted that Hope was her daughter.

If she loved him and trusted him as she'd said she did, why hadn't she, especially now?

Chance tried putting that particular worry out of mind. It was something they could discuss at length later, once the little girl was safe.

Besides, they'd hardly spoken at all since leaving the corral—they'd been moving too fast.

Knowing they should stop to rest and eat competed with the weather front that finally had arrived. It had showered once, and he'd pulled the rain ponchos out of a saddle bag, but by the time they'd donned them, the spurt was over. More rain—a thunderstorm—was coming, though.

Dark clouds had punched their way through the sky and hung ominously overhead. Humidity thickened every breath he took. And thunder rumbled ever closer.

Fearing the kidnappers' tracks would wash away with a heavy rain, he prayed they caught up to them soon.

He would do anything, give anything, to see Hope in Pru's arms, to hear her jabbering in that secret language only a mother seemed to understand fully.

If he thought it would do the trick, he would refuse to testify and go to jail if necessary. But he didn't trust someone who would kidnap a child to play fair.

There being no guarantees made going after Hope a no-brainer.

But assuming they caught up to the kidnappers, Chance knew he would have a serious choice to make. He was uncertain if he should try to overpower them or try to bribe them into cooperating.

He would give up every cent he had to get Hope back, but would it be enough?

He didn't know if he could outbid Moreno and Tunney to buy the kidnappers' allegiance.

And what if one of them had a deeper loyalty? A blood relationship?

Money would have no bearing on what they would do then.

So he would leave bribery as his second choice, Chance decided, and would use as a last resort refusing to testify.

"Haven't we been this way before?" Pru suddenly asked, snapping him out of his reverie. She slowed the chestnut and pointed off to the right. "That odd rock formation looks familiar."

Chance pulled on his reins. The roan danced some but held her ground. He stood in the saddle and made a 240-degree sweep, taking in other familiar points.

"Yeah, looks like they're snaking around."

"On purpose? Do you think they spotted us?"

"More likely they're not so familiar with this country and are finding their way to wherever they're headed. I don't believe they'd even think we would set out after them. Sensible people either would have called in the law…or met their demand."

A sensible man wouldn't have walked out of a hospital without a doctor's approval.

Every now and then his heart beat a little too fast, indicative of the stress he was putting on his exhausted body. And his shoulder was becoming an intrusion. For the past hour or so he'd been trying to ignore the ache. But it was getting deeper, more insistent. The exit wound was kicking up, and he feared it might be infected.

As they started off again, Pru asked, "Do you think we're gaining on them?"

She sounded as exhausted as he felt.

"Hard to say, but I expect so."

Chance eyed the sky just as thunder cracked and a streak of lightning split the cloud bank overhead. The *pit-pat* of raindrops hitting rock surrounded them. Quickly he donned his poncho. Pru did the same.

But this time the rain wasn't just a light shower and it didn't subside. With each minute that passed, the downpour grew heavier, drenching all in its path, sending a steady rivulet along the path they were following. Chance acknowledged they needed to take shelter. Heavy rains could be dangerous in this country.

A wall of rock a few minutes ride to the south looked promising.

Slowing, he turned to Pru. "Let's head over to that overhang."

Exhaustion warring with disappointment in her face, she nodded in agreement. "And pray the rain stops soon."

Knowing she feared losing the kidnappers' trail— a real possibility—Chance chose to put a positive spin to the setback. "They'll have to stop, too, and I don't think they're very far ahead of us."

"I hope you're right."

"Don't worry," he said with false bravado, "their prints will be easy to follow in damp earth."

*If* he could find them in the first place.

# Chapter Eleven

The moment her butt hit the bedroll, Pru allowed the exhaustion to take hold of her. Sitting cross-legged, she closed her eyes for a moment and imagined Hope clinging to her, the little head resting in the hollow between her shoulder and neck. Too, she imagined Chance part of this picture—chest bare and pressed to her back, hand forward and his beard-roughened cheek resting against the side of her face, his long hair tangling with hers, protective arms surrounding them both with warmth and contentment.

*She had to tell him…*

"Hey, go ahead and lie down," Chance said. He was tending to the horses, loosening their cinches. "Get some sleep if you want. I'll wake you when the rain stops."

"Just for a few minutes," she agreed as thunder rumbled deep and threatening.

It didn't sound as though the storm would let up soon.

Pru slid to her side and watched Chance move around the shelter, which had turned out to be a widemouthed, shallow cave with room enough to spread out both bedrolls, build a fire and leave a spacious standing area for their mounts. Though she'd donned her poncho the moment the rain began, Pru felt damp and chilled to the bone. And, as if Chance instinctively sensed that, he gathered a few logs and set them in the remains of the previous fire.

He pulled out a pack of matches and expertly started a small blaze that immediately began to warm her. He'd freed his long hair to dry it.

Licking her lips, she quickly looked away, staring through the downpour curtaining the cave's mouth, and wondered how soon it would let up...wondered whether Chance really would be able to pick up the outlaws' trail as he'd assured her...wondered whether her daughter was dry and warm and safe....

Though she squeezed her eyes shut against threatening tears, they oozed through her lashes and down her cheeks. She began to cry softly, but choked back the sobs that threatened to escape her, lest she add to Chance's burden.

What had she done wrong that Hope was in such danger?

A mother was supposed to protect her child. In that, she had failed miserably, Pru acknowledged. Her fault. Surely she could have been smarter.

Not brought Hope to the hospital in the first place.

Not revealed her daughter's paternity to the kidnappers.

*They knew...Chance didn't....*

Guilt swamped her.

*She had to find a way to tell him!*

A soft touch on her cheek startled her. Eyes flying open, breath lost, she looked into the face she had loved for so long, now the battered and bruised mockery of male beauty.

"Hungry?" he asked, giving her a crooked grin that made her want to cry again.

"Chance…"

*She had to tell him.*

He was sitting next to her and setting down the bag she'd taken from the bunkhouse. "The food you brought is a regular feast."

As he foraged through it, she noticed his movement was unnatural. Stiff. She thought maybe he'd pulled out his shoulder again.

No…wrong shoulder.

"Chance, what's wrong?"

Then it hit her. The exit wound!

She sat up fast. Too fast. Light-headed from lack of food, she faltered and caught herself, leaning forward on her hands. By the time her head cleared and her senses sharpened, Chance was pressing a piece of sausage to her lips.

"Eat."

She wanted to protest, to reveal the thing that had been between them unspoken for too long, but her stomach growled. The food was too seductive. Taking the sausage from his fingers, she was not unaware of the warmth of his flesh touching her lips.

Nothing had ever tasted so good.

Chance had laid out the food next to his bedroll and was using his knife to cut the sausage and cheese and bread into easily edible portions.

"Everything will look better, feel more possible, on a full stomach," he promised.

They ate in silence, washing down the food with water from the canteens. An ordinary task, but under the circumstances, so intimate.

Pru kept her eye on Chance's shoulder. His movements remained unnatural. The wound needed tending. She regretted not having her first aid kit with her.

She regretted a lot of things.

But her not telling him about Hope hadn't been based on a whim. If he had come back anytime during her pregnancy...anytime during the first few months of their daughter's life...she would have told him. She wanted to tell him now. But she also wanted to understand.

"Chance, why did you leave last time?" she asked, hoping for a straight answer.

"Same as always." He popped the last piece of sausage into his mouth. "Itchy feet."

He didn't look at her as he chewed, and Pru knew he'd given her an excuse rather than an explanation.

"And that's why you stayed away for so long?" When he continued to avoid her gaze, she said, "Chance, please, the truth. I need to hear it."

His jaw tightened, and she feared he would give her a flippant answer—his specialty.

"I was afraid," he said when he finally faced her.

"Afraid of what?" she asked, astonished.

"Of you."

"But I loved you!"

"And you were getting these nesting instincts—I could sense it more and more those last weeks we were together." He took a deep breath. "As for me—"

"You weren't ready to make a commitment."

"Not the forever-after kind, and that's what you deserved." He shook his head. "I didn't know if I would ever be ready. So you scared me, and I took off. I wanted to come back so many times. I thought about you, Pru. Constantly. You were always in my head. When I'd win a competition, I'd do it for you." A strange expression clouded his features. "Maybe for us…maybe for that future I knew you wanted and deserved. I never could put it into the proper words."

Stunned as she realized that he'd been trying to prove himself, she said, "I never knew."

His gaze locked onto hers as he said, "I always thought that one day I'd get ready to ride a bronc and I'd look out into the audience and there you'd be, waiting to see me ride and cheer me on."

She'd done that before.

*Before Hope.*

"And then when you never showed," he continued, "I got scared again. I thought I'd done it at last, that I'd driven you away for good."

Hearing this took away her breath. He'd been caught up in trying to deal with a lifelong insecurity, alone.

"Why couldn't you have just picked up a phone and asked me directly?" she demanded, angry for the time they'd wasted. "And don't tell me it isn't your style!"

Chance shrugged, the gesture helpless—a word she never thought she would use to describe him.

"I couldn't believe you loved me that way," he said, "the forever-after kind. I wanted you to, but—"

"You were afraid I'd walk out on you like your mother did to you and your father."

"Pa never got over it. I wouldn't, either."

"So you left first, even though you didn't really want to." She scooted closer to him so she could touch his face and tell him at last. "Chance Quarrels, you're a complicated man. But you're the only man

I've ever loved. The only man I've ever wanted to be with. I waited for you—''

He cut off her passionate declaration with a kiss that started gentle and sweet but quickly built to hard and fierce.

Pru let herself go. She wanted this man, had always wanted him. Kissing him, touching him made her feel better for a while. Made her forget...

Instinctively remembering his musculature, how the heat of his flesh felt against hers, she slid her hands along his arms and up his chest. The texture was exactly as she imagined it. Her fingertips burned with wanting more. When her hand neared his left shoulder, though, he flinched.

Abruptly she pulled away. The wound. She'd nearly forgotten.

''I'm sorry. Take off your shirt, Chance, please. Let me see how bad it is.''

He did as she demanded without argument, his movements halting and obviously filled with pain. Pru swallowed hard. The area around the exit wound had collapsed into angry, red, receding flesh. The opening itself oozed a bit, though she knew it could be worse.

''Double damnation, it is infected.''

''I kinda figured that,'' Chance said.

''Then why didn't you say something?''

''Didn't seem important in the grand scheme of things.''

''Of course it's important,'' she muttered. ''You're important.''

Somehow he'd never figured that out. His father had never made him feel that way, nor had his brothers. And obviously she, too, had failed him.

A sin of omission was sometimes the most destructive where emotional lives were involved.

Taking a deep breath, she said, "That wound needs treatment. You didn't by any chance stuff a first aid kid in those saddle bags?"

"Nope. But I did find this in one of them."

He reached over and picked up a pint bottle of tequila that was still half-full. She took it from him, grateful for small favors.

"It'll do."

Unfortunately she had no sterile pads. No tape. Could make no dressing to protect him. She would have to improvise. Make do with what she had.

To that purpose she reached for the cloth bag that had held their food and said, "I need your knife."

"Can I trust you?" he teased, handing over the weapon.

The trust comment getting to her, Pru couldn't look at him. "I'll do my best."

After cutting the bag into cloth strips, she folded one into a pad and doused it with tequila, making sure not to waste any of the precious alcohol. It would have to last until they could get Chance back to civilization.

"One favor," Chance requested as she was about to clean the wound. "Don't tell me this is gonna hurt you more than it does me."

Always joking, even in the face of pain, she thought. "I don't want to hurt you, Chance."

Not any more than she already had. Or would when she finally told him that she had given birth to his child and had never told him.

"I know you don't, Prunella. I should have known

it all along—you would never do anything to hurt me.''

Heart in her throat, Pru slid her eyes away from his. She concentrated on the wound, gently dabbing as Chance sat rigid, his jaw clenched tight. He didn't utter a sound as she removed the infected matter.

Stoic, that's what he was—a man who hid his pain by ignoring it. Or by resorting to charm and humor to cover up. And he'd never failed to show a worse side of himself whenever it had been expected of him.

*Was his leaving her fault, then?* she wondered.

Pru suspected so. Her nesting instincts might have scared Chance—and rightly so, since she had been pregnant, albeit unknowingly at the time. But she imagined the reason for his actions went even deeper. Part of her had expected him to leave. Had expected him to abandon her, even though he'd finally told her he loved her.

And so he'd left.

Once more, Chance Quarrels had fulfilled the negative prophecy surrounding him ever since his mother Sunny had walked away from the Curly-Q and out of his life.

Pru tore her thoughts from a past that couldn't be changed and concentrated on the present. All she could do was manage the present right now, one moment at a time. And once they had Hope safe, she would see to the future.

"It's looking better already," she murmured. The tequila bottle in hand, she said, "Hang in there just a minute longer. Don't move."

Tipping the bottle, Pru allowed a bit of the alcohol to drip directly into the raw flesh. Chance's jaw clenched tighter, if that was possible, but he didn't make a sound, didn't move an inch.

Pru's heart went out to him. "I'm sorry I couldn't make it feel better," she murmured as she screwed the cap back on the bottle.

"You make me feel better, Pru…" Lifting his un-injured arm, Chance used a finger to push a stray strand of hair from her forehead. "Whenever I'm around you."

Heart thudding at the soft touch, she pleaded, "Then don't go away anymore."

"I may have to. You know that. If I need to pull out of the trial to get Hope back for you, I will. Who knows what the authorities will do to me then."

Jail. He meant being incarcerated. He was willing to do that for her. For a child that she loved. Her emotions threatened to overwhelm her.

"Shh." She put a finger to his lips. "Don't say that. You're not going to jail. You're going to pick up those tracks, and we're going to find the kidnappers and get Hope back. And then everything will be all right."

"Everything," he agreed.

*Now,* she thought… "But about the last time you were gone, Chance, there's something I have to tell you."

She had to be honest with him before they caught up to the outlaws. Before one of them threw the truth about Hope in Chance's face.

"No, you don't, Miss Prudence. You don't have to tell me anything," he insisted, sliding his arms around her and drawing her close. "Just love me now. That's all I ask."

"I do love you, Chance. I have forever. And I will forever after, I promise."

"Forever after," he murmured, dipping his head to kiss her again.

Intense emotions roiling in her, Pru tried to show him how much and how deeply she loved him and believed in him. She couldn't think straight, couldn't pull herself free from the sweet fantasy.

He would get their daughter back...then she would tell him...and they would be a family at last.

Reminding herself that he never disappointed expectations, Pru would expect only the best from Chance, and then he would give it to her.

The steady drum of rain became hypnotic background music to their embrace...*pit-pat, pit-pat, pit-pat*...soothing and seductive.

Chance released her mouth. "Ah, Miss Prudence, you can't know how much I want you...need you," he murmured.

"Have me, then, Chance. Take what you need."

Pru needed Chance, as well, not only to fulfill her, but to keep her strong. The two of them together as one could beat any odds, she told herself. They could get their daughter back unharmed.

Chance didn't hesitate at the invitation, but began to undress her, starting with her boots. When he removed her socks and scraped a thumbnail along the ball of one foot. Her toes curled at the sensation that swept through her entire body.

Breath catching, she lay back on her elbows. By firelight, she watched him drag down her jeans and panties in one smooth sweep and toss them to the side. Then he nestled his head between her thighs to kiss them open. Golden reflections of the flames danced along his nude torso as his tongue touched her, explored the lushness of her so that her hips tilted for him without her conscious thought.

And when he slid back up along her belly, she took his tongue eagerly in her mouth, tasting both of them together.

Together...the way it should be between them.

Without breaking the kiss, Chance slid a hand between them, cupped her breast, molding it, fitting it to his palm before moving on to undo the buttons down the center.

At the same time, she worked a hand between their hips so she could unsnap and unzip his jeans, then search for him as she'd ached to do for so long.

''Miss Prudence!''

The words exploded into her mouth as she found him, hot and heavy and ready. With her free hand, she tugged at the back of his jeans, slid her hand into the loosened material and pressed her fingertips into his flesh in the same rhythm. He moaned in her mouth and she went back to the jeans, wanting to free him completely. Wanting to take him inside her. He had to help her work the garment down to his knees.

Finally she broke the kiss. Unable to wait longer, she urged him, ''Now!''

Hips tilting, she received him, the path primed slick to ease his entry. He slid into her as though it hadn't been more than two years. Wanting him inside her deeper, as if that could imprint him on her soul, she eased her thighs upward and wrapped her legs along his back, then tangled her fingers in his long hair to urge him on.

With a groan Chance pushed her blouse free from

her breasts and nipped at her flesh through her bra until her nipples stood out, firm points that begged for suckling. Chance did so and Pru felt as if her heart flowed out to him though her breasts, as if their souls touched inside her.

The two of them together...one...forever after.

For now she could pretend.

Could indulge in the fantasy.

Could lose herself in the man she loved at least for a little while.

Because deep inside herself Pru feared she had made a terrible mistake in hiding the truth about their child from Chance...one that he might never fully forgive.

CHANCE STARTED AWAKE.

What had disturbed him? Holding his breath, he listened intently.

Nothing.

That was it. The constant drumming was no more. The area outside the cave was wreathed in a wet gloom, but the rain had stopped.

"Pru," he said softly, but she was sound asleep, one arm raised over her head, her naked breasts gleaming pale and alluring in the low light.

He wanted to make love to her anew. To exhaust both of them yet again. But a more important mission roused him from their cozy, makeshift bed.

Hope. The daughter of the woman he loved.

The cave was still warm, though the logs were mere embers. Still, Chance covered Pru before pulling on his jeans and boots. Then he stood over her, content to watch her sleep for a moment longer.

Earlier, Pru had been trying to tell him about the

circumstances of Hope's birth. He hadn't wanted her to think that she had to explain how things had been for her when he'd left. Or to hold herself accountable when he didn't.

He held himself accountable, though.

For the bank robbery…the security guard's death…endangering Pru's life…now Hope's…

The Cowboy Poet had him nailed. Chance would do anything for Pru or someone dear to her.

"Pru, it's time to go," he called softly.

But still she didn't stir.

Her breath came deep and steady. Her features were relaxed for the first time since they had started out. Her whole body appeared fluid. He couldn't bear to wake her again, to see the heartbreak etched on the face so dear to him when she thought of Hope's plight.

Sleep was allowing her to heal.

*Heal…his shoulder.*

He took a moment to douse the wound with tequila. The flesh there might not look as bad as it had earlier, but it felt worse as he pulled on his shirt. He resheathed the knife and grabbed the slicker.

Without Pru, he would move faster, Chance reasoned, he'd find those tracks more easily if she wasn't distracting him. Then, when he had good news, he would come back for her, and together they would rescue her daughter.

After tightening the roan's cinch, he swung up into the saddle and looked back at his love, still breathing deeply, still sound asleep.

"I'll come back for you, Pru," he promised before riding off into the mist.

THE LACK OF A WARM BODY to snuggle up to awoke Pru.

"Mmm...Chance?" she called softly, feeling the empty place next to her.

No answer.

Yawning, Pru frowned and sat up groggily, forcing her eyes open. She took in her surroundings, gradually remembering where she was and why.

Then, with a flash it hit her—the rain had stopped.

"Chance!" she called, now excited.

But he didn't respond. His things were gone, including his horse.

Chest squeezing tight, Pru knew a moment's panic.

Chance had gone off without her. Without a word.

Again.

## Chapter Twelve

Chance hadn't expected that picking up the trail would be so easy. He'd found it within minutes of arriving at the place where he and Pru had cut over toward the cave. Continuing along the same route brought him to a steep rise.

Once he'd crested it, the trail was obvious. The kidnappers had followed the natural path that cut through a densely forested area. Their horses' tracks intermingled with those of deer and other wildlife, and Chance figured it was a regular route to a water source.

He should go back and get Pru now, but Chance was torn between doing so and going a bit farther to see how things played out.

Just a few more minutes...

A short trek brought him to the edge of a clearing, where he could see a log cabin perched alongside a stream—that local water source he'd expected to find. Movement caught his attention. Horses grazed in the meadow. And beyond them, close to the cabin, a big man chopped wood.

One of the kidnappers?

Gut tightening, Chance patted the roan's neck and

murmured, "Easy, girl," hoping he could get closer without her giving away the game.

Keeping to the shadows of the green belt, he took the mare around the edge of the clearing until he was almost directly behind the woodpile, where he spotted a late-model SUV.

And then he heard a wail issue from within the cabin—clearly a young child.

*Hope!*

Certain of it, Chance decided that he couldn't go back for Pru, after all. Not now. Not when he was so close. Not when the outlaws had the means for easy escape in a four-wheel-drive vehicle. He would have to do this himself. Hopefully, surprise would be on his side.

Chance saw his opportunity for redemption. He could make certain that no one else was hurt. He could prove his devotion to the woman he loved. As for Pru herself being left out of the picture—when she had her child back safe and sound in her arms, nothing else would matter to her.

Chance freed the rifle from the saddle holster and judged the possibility of a successful ambush. Fifty-fifty at best, but he was willing to try for it.

Dismounting, he crept forward.

The horses in the meadow got wind of him and became edgy. One whinnied and snorted.

Continuing to split firewood, however, the man didn't seem to notice.

His rifle pointed at the broad back, Chance thought quickly. He didn't want to shoot, not because the bastard didn't deserve being blown away for what he'd done, but because he himself was no killer. Even wounding the man to take him out of the equation wasn't to his taste. Besides which, the crack of a rifle shot would be sharp and distinctive. The woman inside would hear it, even over Hope's continuing cries.

He would have to sneak in close enough to knock the man over the head, Chance decided.

Stealth wasn't his long suit—he held his breath as he edged closer, stepping in rhythm with the ax splitting wood. The ground beneath his boots was porous, and already signs of the recent rain were receding. He'd nearly gotten within striking distance when the man suddenly whirled on him and heaved a log so fast that Chance didn't have time to duck.

Wood hit metal, and the rifle popped out of Chance's hands, the barrel striking his bad shoulder before flying off to the side. The pain stunned him long enough for the kidnapper to take the advantage. Chance hardly had time to assimilate the leathery skin, dark eyes and drooping mustache, before enduring another blow that sent him sprawling to the ground, his heart pounding in a strange rhythm.

The man was on him.

Wounded shoulder shrieking in protest, Chance grabbed his attacker's shirtfront with both fists and did a back roll in the wet grass. His assailant came with him and flew over his head.

In a flash they were both on their feet, squaring off. Chance recognized the man, who worked for a company that supplied bulls at rodeos—Ray somebody or other.

"You're on private land here!" Ray growled.

Heartbeat normalizing, Chance asked, "How much are Tunney and Moreno paying you?"

The man straightened and spat a chaw of tobacco

on the ground between them. "Don't know what you mean."

"Sure you don't. And that little girl in the cabin is yours—isn't she, Ray?" When the man appeared surprised, Chance said, "Yeah, that's right. I recognize you. Only I didn't know you were friends with bank robbers."

"I'm not."

"Strictly a cash transaction for you, then," Chance mused, playing for time. He wasn't as fit as he'd like to be—that strange heartbeat coming and going kept him on edge. "What about the woman?"

"What about me?"

The voice slid down Chance's spine like raw silk. Turning, he gaped at the big-haired blonde who'd left the cabin and was training a six-shooter and brown doe eyes, lashes thick with mascara, on him.

"Silky...you?" He couldn't believe the rodeo groupie was one of the kidnappers.

"Me, Chance."

"Why?"

"It's not personal. I got nothin' against you...although there was that one time I did try..." she said suggestively.

The Arena, Chance remembered. The night of the bank robbery.

Silky had wanted him because he'd been the big winner. She collected winners—ones willing to show her around in style. Obviously this time she'd decided to win big for herself.

Time for plan B.

He asked, "So how much are the two of you being paid to carry this off?"

"Enough," Ray stated.

"How about more?"

"You, Chance?" Silky asked, sounding surprised. "You have that kind of money?"

"I've won some good purses in the last couple of years, and I haven't had a reason to spend much of it. I can afford you, darlin'."

"Sounds interesting," Ray said.

But after taking a moment to think over his offer, Silky shook her head. "No."

"Why not?" her partner asked. "He's seen us. He knows who we are now."

"That's right. And that's really too bad. Get his rifle, Ray."

As her partner went for the weapon, Silky wrapped both hands around the handgun to better aim it. Chance glimpsed the gold and diamond ring she wore—big enough to split his lip.

But was Silky strong enough to land the punch that had done it? he wondered.

"I always did cotton to you, Chance," Silky purred, regret in her voice.

"Then you won't do anything foolish."

"Foolish would be letting you go," she said. "Foolish would be going to jail 'cause I let you sweet-talk me. This way you won't be talkin' to anyone. And, after all, that's the point of this whole set up, isn't it?"

Sweat popping along his skin, Chance thought to stall, thought to formulate a plan C that would actually work. "So why didn't you just kill me when you had the chance in that alley the other night?"

An odd expression crossed Silky's features, but she quickly recovered. "We're done with talking here. Ray, go ahead and shoot him."

"Me? I didn't sign on to kill no one."

"So you'll get a bonus!" she snapped. "Kidnapping is a federal offense, you idiot. What do you think will happen to us if he talks?"

Suddenly a shot whined through the clearing, making them all start.

On instinct Chance lunged forward and tackled the blonde. The handgun exploded but the shot went wild. He twisted it out of her hand, but before he could recoup, Ray whacked him with his own rifle, and pain blazed through his shoulder. Chance spun around and stumbled to his knees.

"Stop right there, both of you!" came Pru's shout. "Drop that rifle, mister, or I'll shoot to kill!"

Chance had never seen such a beautiful sight as his red-haired tigress walking toward them on the chestnut, across the meadow, her rifle shouldered and aimed in their direction.

"Don't believe it," Silky told her partner. "The preacher's daughter isn't gonna shoot no one."

"Maybe not," Pru said. "But the outraged, grief-stricken mother just might."

Ray dropped the rifle.

"Where is she?" Pru demanded, her voice choked. "What have you done with my little girl?"

"Hope's inside," Chance told Pru as he stuffed the handgun in his belt and picked up the rifle.

Not taking her eyes off the kidnappers, Pru asked, "Is she all right?"

"She'd better be," Chance said, suddenly aware of the silence—Hope had stopped crying.

"Nothing wrong with your kid except maybe she's a little dehydrated from all that bawling," Silky muttered.

"I'm closer. I'll get her." Chance started backing toward the cabin, barely a dozen yards away now. Then to Silky and Ray, "You two, get on your stomachs before I shoot you." He'd carry through with the threat if they forced his hand.

As they both went down to the ground, Pru dismounted and shouldered the rifle. "I've got them covered."

"If one of them twitches," Chance told her, "shoot."

He whipped into the cabin, whose interior was dark but for the gloom creeping through the windows.

"Hope," he said, keeping his voice low and reassuring, while inside, his gut was churning.

It took his eyes a minute to adjust before he spotted the door to another room. Quickly he opened it, his heart again racing unnaturally.

But the beat evened out when he spotted Hope safe in a cot, sound asleep, her little chest rising and falling naturally. She seemed unharmed, though her cheeks were streaked with dried tears. Setting down the rifle, he scooped her up in his arms, the movement enough to arouse her.

Her eyes blinked opened and met his...and Chance got the oddest feeling....

She frowned, and for a moment Chance feared she would start crying again. Then she smiled and smacked him in the nose and made a hoarse demand. "M'ma!"

Only this time Chance understood that she wasn't asking for food—she wanted her mother.

"Yeah, Squirt, Mama's here," he murmured, kissing her cheek. Tasting the salt of her tears made him want to make someone pay. He kept himself calm for her sake. ''C'mon, let's go see your mama.''

He grabbed his rifle on the way out of the room.

Once outside the cabin he yelled, ''She's okay, Pru!'' then hesitated a second.

Some instinct made him look real deep into the little girl's blue eyes...something he'd never before done...and what he saw there stunned him more thoroughly than any hit he could take.

PRU WEPT WITH RELIEF the moment Chance put Hope in her trembling arms. She hugged her daughter tight and silently vowed never to let anything bad happen to her again.

''Ah, Hope, sweetheart,'' she sniffed, ''I was so scared...so scared...but now you're safe.''

She kissed Hope's face all over until the child squirmed in her arms and squealed in protest. ''M'ma, no!'' While she clung to Pru's neck and curled a leg around her side, she hid her face from her mother's attention.

''It's all right, Squirt, it's all right,'' she murmured, picking up on the nickname Chance had given her.

Through her tears Pru watched him stand guard over the kidnappers, who remained facedown on the ground. His stance stiff, he seemed to be ignoring her.

No doubt he was still shocked by the fact that Hope was her child....

He'd muttered, ''Here's your mama,'' had set Hope in her arms, then had turned his back on them both. Well, she had a bone to pick with him, too. How dare he scare her the way he had, making her think he'd deserted her? Even now she felt the remains of the anger and desperation she'd experienced when she'd found him gone.

She'd left the cave as fast as possible. Luckily, the rain had made his tracks easy to follow, and realizing he'd gone after Hope without her, she'd been determined to catch up as fast as she could.

She'd done so and just in time...not that Chance seemed in the least grateful.

Suddenly he whistled, the eerie sound disturbing the horses, the two in the meadow and hers. A movement caught her eye and she turned to see the blue roan step from the tree line. Chance repeated the sound, urging the mare to pick up her hooves and move toward him with purpose.

"Get the rope, would you, Pru," he said, his tone flat.

"All right."

Without taking her gaze from the devils who had stolen her child from her, she went for the mare. Lifting the coil of rope off the saddle horn, she slid it over her arm and brought it to Chance.

Who avoided looking directly at her as he took it and threw it in front of the woman.

"C'mon, Silky, get up and tie Ray's hands behind his back, nice and tight."

The blonde quickly did as he ordered, asking, "I don't suppose I could find a way to make you forget I was involved in this, Chance, darlin'?"

"You suppose right. Back on your stomach and don't so much as twitch," he warned. He asked Pru, "Can you hold Hope and keep them covered?"

"I can do whatever is necessary," she promised.

He laid his rifle out of reach and crouched down,

settling one knee in the middle of Silky's back. Rather than cut the rope, he merely gave it some slack, then tied her hands so the two kidnappers were linked together. Next he lifted one of her legs and secured an ankle, after which he did the same to the man he'd called Ray.

"You're gonna regret this, Chance," Ray muttered.

"It's you two who are going to do all the regretting."

The realization that Chance knew the villains finally sank in as he finished trussing them as if for a branding. Rage replacing the relief she'd felt at being reunited with Hope, Pru only wished she had a hot iron in hand....

Chance leaned over and patted down Ray. He stuck a hand in the man's pocket and pulled out a set of keys.

"I'll be right back," he said, without actually turning toward her. "Watch 'em close."

Still he looked straight ahead as he stalked off. Pru vacillated between disappointment and anger. She had her own issues with him, but now that Hope was safe, they were deflating like the air leaving a balloon.

Having caught a glimpse of a vehicle, she figured he was going to fetch it. And she was thankful they wouldn't have to go home the way they'd come. She'd had enough horseback riding for a while.

It was all accomplished in a few minutes—securing the kidnappers in the back of the vehicle, relieving the horses of their tack so they could graze freely until someone came to get them, settling in with

Hope sleeping in her lap—of course Silky and Ray hadn't provided a car seat for the child.

Then Pru noticed the cell phone. "Chance, my God, a telephone!"

"How thoughtful."

He picked it up and nodded appreciatively at the captors turned captives.

Still, she and he weren't connecting, Pru realized, growing anxious at the thought.

She didn't say a word as he thoughtfully stared at the cell phone in his hand. Nor when he punched a couple of buttons and put it to his ear. He seemed to be listening. Suddenly his eyes narrowed and his jaw clenched.

"What?" a confused Pru asked. "What's going on?"

"That's what I'd like to know," Chance muttered.

The end of his dialogue with her. He shut off the phone and without another word drove off. And somehow Pru was left with a creeping sense of guilt.

He was angry with her, and she could only think of one reason...he *knew*.

At last he'd come face-to-face with the truth—that Hope was their daughter—and it hadn't come from her. His being angry was natural. And temporary.

It would be all right, she told herself. She'd make it all right.

A dirt road took them to a gravel one, the gravel to a third that was paved. Within minutes they passed a highway sign, and Chance flipped open the cell phone again. This time he dialed a series of numbers.

"Felice, it's me." He paused to listen. "We got her, and she's fine. We're on our way in now, with the kidnappers in tow.'' Another pause. ''No. A vehicle.''

Pru only half listened as he pinpointed their location as best he could and asked whether someone was available to go find Bart, who apparently was on the trail after them.

To her he said nothing.

Pru's heart squeezed tight, and she clung to the child that would connect them always.


A WELCOMING COMMITTEE was waiting for them when they got back to the Curly-Q—Emmett, Felice, Moon-Eye, Bart and Josie, Daniel and Lainey. All rushed out of the house before Chance could even stop the SUV. No Kleef or Will, he noticed as he slid from behind the driver's seat.

Felice flew at him. ''My Chance, are you all right?'' she asked, hands fluttering over him as if she could ascertain his physical condition by touch.

He gave her a one-armed hug. ''Reasonable,'' he said, grateful for the comfort she gave him.

He wasn't about to mention the occasional irregular heartbeat or the shoulder that hurt like hell. She'd be calling for the paramedics again.

He looked around at the lot of them, each and every one appearing concerned. His niece appeared ready to cry, and for once, instead of torturing her, his nephew stood with his arm around his sister, acting the protective big brother. Part of a family pulling together.

For him, Chance realized in amazement.

''What in tarnation is going on?'' Emmett demanded, breaking the spell. ''What's this about kidnappers?''

"Long story, Pa."

"So give me the short version."

Exhausted, Chance pulled himself together. The night was going to be a long one, he feared.

"I'm scheduled to testify in a trial on Monday. The two trussed up like a couple of heifers in the back of that vehicle were trying to see that I don't."

Bombarded by a myriad of questions, he said, "Later, please."

"A curse on anyone who would hold a child to do this terrible thing!" Felice muttered, turning her attention to Pru, who stood near the vehicle with Hope.

Chance stared at the child, who sucked her thumb and curled in closer to her mother. His heart melted every time he looked at her.

*How could he have been so blind?*

He turned his back on Pru again.

Bart was saying, "I called Sheriff Malone, and he agreed that I should bring the kidnappers in."

Chance knew his brother had merely taken a long leave from his job and was still officially a deputy—if of another county. "Good."

"Come inside," Felice urged them. "I have food."

"No food," Pru said. "I...I think we'd like to go home."

Though he was still avoiding direct contact, Chance felt her eyes on him, pleading with him. "Fine," he said. "I'll take you."

"Whoa." Bart was shaking his head. "No one's going anywhere until I get your statements."

"That can wait a few minutes." Josie stepped into the fray and put an arm around Pru. "Come inside

and sit down. You look worn-out. And you might
not be hungry, but what about Hope?''

"She could use a change," Pru said, "but I didn't
think to get her diaper bag."

"So we'll improvise."

"We have lots of dish towels and safety pins,"
Felice added. "Perhaps you would let me take care
of the little one?"

"Sure."

"And I can help," Lainey offered, tagging along
with the women as they headed inside.

Wanting to get the whole thing over with, to have
some peace and just be alone inside his head, Chance
felt the situation spinning out of his control.

"Pa, maybe you'd better go in, too." This from
Bart.

"I already ate."

"Then go rest." Bart's voice tightened with authority. "We wouldn't want to overtax your heart,
now, would we?"

The two men glared at each other, and to Chance's
amazement, Bart won. Without another word their
father stalked off and into the house.

"Uh, I'll be inside, too, Dad." Daniel backed off
warily. "Unless you need me."

"Go ahead, son."

Bart walked over to the back of the SUV and
opened it. He officially arrested Silky and Ray, who
still lay trussed up in the back. He even read them
their rights.

Then he turned to the hired hand. "Moon-Eye,
could you cover these two for a few minutes?"

"My pleasure." Moon-Eye grinned and fondled
the rifle he was carrying. "Maybe they'll try to get

away. I've always gotten a bang outta varmint hunting.''

Bart indicated Chance should follow him. Knowing what was coming, he nevertheless followed his brother all the way to the corral. He couldn't stall any longer.

Bart didn't disappoint him. ''So what's the rest of the story? And I suggest you don't leave anything out.''

Chance told him everything, from the joke about robbing a bank gone bad to Pru's riding to his rescue.

''Got yourself in quite a fix this time, little brother,'' Bart mused.

''I don't need a lecture right now.''

''I wasn't going to give you one. I was going to offer you a hand. I'm wondering why you didn't ask for one in the first place. I'm wondering why you never ask your family for anything.''

''Hard to ask, when your family doesn't think much of you.''

''Hard to think much of a man who seems to want to be at odds with the world.''

''Not the world. Mostly Pa and you,'' Chance admitted. ''You always know what's best. Always did, even when we were kids. When your ma died and you came to live here with us, you proved that. You just up and took over...second only to Pa, that is.''

''That's what Pa wanted. What he expected of me.''

''Did you ever think of what we wanted or expected—Reed and me? Especially Reed.''

''You were just boys.''

''And you weren't?'' Chance's shoulder was

throbbing to an inner beat, not unlike an abscessed tooth.

"Reed never complained."

"Reed never complains about anything!" Chance countered. "He was the heir apparent to the spread until you came along and ruined everything. The spread was his life then. It was his world. But Reed being who he is just swallowed his resentment and disappointment and did as he was told even when his own knowledge and experience and natural savvy were superior to yours! And why? Out of respect. Just because that's how Pa wanted it."

"That was between Reed and me, Chance."

"But Reed wasn't one to stir up grief."

"So you did?"

"I was angry for him, okay? You were the outsider, but Pa pushed you on us," Chance stated, remembering as if it had just happened. "Reed and I were close until you moved in."

Then Reed had become their older brother's shadow, and Chance had somehow gotten lost in the shuffle. Pa had never paid him any mind, that was for certain. Except to yell at him, of course.

"Is that why you made so much trouble for me?" Bart mused. "Because you figured you lost the only brother you wanted to have in your life?"

"It was more complicated than that, Bart. I was doing it for him." No matter that Reed had told him to quit numerous times.

And Bart seemed never to have caught on to why they were always at odds.

"I see."

But Chance wondered if he really did. At least he'd spoken his mind at last.

Whatever Bart thought of the admission, he put it aside to take Chance's official statement. And then they walked back to the ranch house together. Bart went inside to talk to Pru, and Chance chose not to accompany him.

Instead, he pulled his truck next to the SUV and cut the engine.

"How's it going, Moon-Eye."

"Them varmints ain't no fun." He gave Chance a thoughtful look. "Oughta check yourself back into that hospital, boy."

"Not if my life depended on it."

"Could be that it will. You let that infection go and you'll be regrettin' it."

"How can you tell the wound's infected?"

"Having only one good eye can be a plus. Sometimes it lets me see things other people are blind to."

Somehow Chance didn't think Moon-Eye was talking strictly about his shoulder.

"As in…?"

"How much you love that girl, for one."

The reminder gave Chance an unpleasant jolt. Heartsick, he said, "Yeah, well, sometimes love isn't all it's cracked up to be."

"Don't be like your pa."

Damn, he wished people would stop saying that! "I'm nothing like Pa."

"Prove it, then," Moon-Eye said. "Don't throw away people just 'cause they don't always meet your good expectations."

The warning gave him a grave amount of discomfort.

They fell into an uneasy quiet.

Chance had too much to think over. He was in no condition to make any decisions.

Exhaustion quickly overtook him. The moment he laid his head back against the seat, his eyelids grew heavy....

AFTER GIVING Bart her statement, Pru climbed into the truck and slammed the door, startling Chance awake. He rustled around in his seat as she managed to secure her seat belt and settle a sleeping Hope in her lap.

He still wasn't talking to her.

Stiffly she said, "I'm ready if you are."

Chance responded by starting the engine. Outside the truck, Bart was checking over the bonds holding the kidnappers.

She heard Bart say, "Moon-Eye, how about riding shotgun for me."

"My pleasure."

The climb out of the canyon was laborious. It dragged on Pru's nerves until she was ready to scream. Chance didn't say a word to her, though she felt his attention was more on her and Hope than on his driving. She feared the washboard road or Chance's stopping on either side of the gate to open and close it might awaken Hope, but the poor baby had exhausted herself and now lay sound asleep as only a child who felt secure could.

"Chance," she finally said, "can we talk about it?"

"Kind of late for talking, isn't it?" he asked, his answering at all surprising her. "You had what? Nearly two and a half years?"

"You weren't here."

"You knew how to find me. You did it before when you wanted to."

"When exactly should I have come looking for you?" Pru asked, trying to contain the resentment and fear that had shadowed her from the day she realized that she was pregnant. "When I was huge with Hope inside me? Or when she was first born and I was struggling, trying to figure out how to handle something I wasn't ready for myself? You said you loved me, Chance, then you up and left me. I thought—"

"The worst, of course. That I had used you. That I lied to get you in bed. Is that what you think of me?"

"You didn't come back! I didn't think I mattered. That maybe that's what you wanted me to think."

Silence hung heavy between them for a moment.

Then he said, "I'm back now. I've been back for days. We've been intimate twice, for God's sake, and still you couldn't find it in you to tell me that Hope was our daughter!"

"I tried!" She had, Pru thought defensively. "Something kept getting in the way."

Fear.

She realized that her putting off telling him had been due to her own deep-seated fear. She hadn't wanted him to disappoint her again.

"Yeah. You put me to the lowest common denominator, just like my family always has. You didn't tell me," Chance said, "because you didn't trust me, not even after what happened between us tonight. Not after all your declarations...or mine."

Pru had no defense. He was right, after all. He'd hit the crux of the matter. She, like his father and

Bart, had always expected him to behave irresponsibly.

Too late had she vowed to change the way she thought.

But there was more to her fears, she realized, not wanting to put voice to the rest.

Unease stretched between them until Chance pulled up in front of her sister's place.

"Hope, honey, we're home," she whispered, adjusting the child so she could get out of the truck.

She opened the door, then hesitated.

Chance obviously had nothing more to say to her.

Pru tried one more time. "You should come in and let me look at that shoulder."

"More magic in your bag of first aid tricks?" he asked, his tone bitter.

"Then see *someone!*"

Hanging on to their daughter, she scrambled from the truck as Justine came running out of the house, followed by Blythe and Fancy and Mitch.

"Thank God you're both safe and sound!" Justine said, throwing her arms around Pru and Hope. "When Felice called to tell us you and Chance had gone after Hope, I thought I might never see either of you again."

"Don't worry, it's over now," Pru told her sister. With tears in her eyes, she watched Chance drive away. "I'm afraid it's *all* over."

## Chapter Thirteen

*It wasn't over....*

Chance knew that as surely as he knew anything. The thought rode him all the way to Doc Baxter's place, where he let the old guy patch him up, shoot him up and give him a handful of little pills that were supposed to keep away the infection and keep him out of pain.

Doc Baxter also advised Chance to get back to the hospital for an electrocardiogram and make certain that his heart was 100 percent, after what he'd been through.

Advice that Chance chose to take with a grain of salt.

*It wasn't over....*

The thought stayed with him all the way home, curled up with him in bed, filtered though his dreams.

He awoke in the middle of the night, sweating over it.

He thought back to Pru's spotting the cell phone in the SUV.

The first call he'd made on instinct. He'd wanted to know who Silky or Ray had been talking to last and so had hit Redial. He'd gotten through to an answering machine. Silky's. Her voice. An obviously new message meant for someone involved in the operation.

"Hope springs eternal," she'd begun with a bubbly laugh.

The common saying was meant to be enigmatic, Chance was certain, Hope referring to his daughter's kidnapping.

"The plan's been altered, but it keeps getting better."

Because they'd figured they really had him, Hope being his kid and all—and him not even knowing it. Then her tone had turned suggestive.

"So let's rodeo, cowboy..."

Cowboy?

The Cowboy Poet?

Who the hell was he?

Not Ray, that was for certain. Not Tunney or Moreno—they were removed from the equation because they couldn't meet Silky anywhere.

What had been in the back of Chance's mind fermenting all along finally became clear. Rumor had it that he'd been involved in the bank robbery. He'd put it to someone's knowing about his instigating the heist.

But maybe not...

No one remembered seeing Tunney and Moreno's old beater around—and it wouldn't have made a reliable getaway car in the first place.

But what if there had been a different car?

What if there had been a getaway driver?

What if there had been a third man?

One who now had lots and lots of money—the bank's funds that had never been recovered....

The Cowboy Poet?

Whoever had left those notes for him—in his gear, on his person, on his hospital tray—had to be somewhere nearby, aware of his every move. That person had to be right here on the Curly-Q Ranch.

So, which one was it—Kleef Hatsfield or Billy-Boy Spencer? An unknown cowpoke who just happened to show up at the right place at the right time? Or an old acquaintance who just happened to be working on the spread when he'd arrived?

Chance was determined to find out. *Now.*

The bunkhouse was quiet and dark as he moved through the common room to the other bunk room. He knocked. No answer. He wasn't surprised. Neither man had been around when he'd rolled in with the kidnappers. Purposely? Had one of the men feared Silky would betray him?

The door swung open easily, and his flipping on the light confirmed the room was empty. Where had the men gone? Why both of them? Too late for Will and Kleef to be hanging out at the Silver Slipper.

Their beds were made, their possessions neatly tucked in drawers and closets.

He checked the closet first. Only a few garments hung there. Certainly neither of them had the wardrobe of a man who was planning to stick around long.

He searched through pockets and checked the shelves overhead for some clue. Some revelation. Anything suspicious.

Nothing.

He went through the bags below.

Empty.

He searched further, going through drawers.

Useless.

Chance even searched the bunks—both men slept in a lower. No luck on the first. As he was going through the second bunk, he glanced up and froze for a moment as he spotted an object foreign to the bed frame and springs.

Chance stood on the lower bunk and lifted the top mattress. Reaching back, he retrieved the object that had been sloppily concealed by the edge of a sheet— a weapon of sorts, one that had been used against him in the mugging.

A cattle prod.

The proof he'd needed that someone on this ranch was responsible might be right here, Chance realized. But which one? Will or Kleef?

On the one hand Will had seemed awfully concerned about his plans to leave the ranch.

On the other, Kleef had disappeared for a while before the stampede, and from what he'd been told, Will had come to Chance's rescue.

Chance didn't have enough to go on to figure it out. Maybe if he faced the men down he could get the guilty one to reveal himself.

But where the hell had they disappeared to? And again, why both of them at the same time? Was it possible they were together? he wondered. He glanced out the window—neither man's vehicle was around.

Thoroughly frustrated, he kicked a nearby wastebasket and sent the contents flying.

"Double damnation!" he growled, echoing Pru.

He grabbed the container and started retrieving the candy wrappers and cigarette packs and discarded wads of paper that littered the floor. As he shoved the refuse back in the basket, one half-crumpled sheet of paper with a graphic of a horse's back hooves flailing caught his eye.

Flattened, the sheet proved to be a flyer advertising a rodeo in Trinity, the place where the whole mess he was in had started. He'd been so wound up these past weeks that he'd plain forgotten that he'd meant to ride in it. The date for the rough stock events was tomorrow.

No, today, Chance amended, realizing the sun would rise in another hour.

*So let's rodeo, cowboy.*

Silky's exact words. Had she planned on meeting the Cowboy Poet in Trinity?

Heart palpitating, Chance ignored the warning.

He knew what he had to do.

PRU ARRIVED at the Curly-Q shortly before noon. She had to talk to Chance. She just had to.

She'd awakened with the certainty that something wasn't right. Nothing she could put her finger on, yet she couldn't dispel her intuition.

Driving straight up to the bunkhouse in her sister's car—her station wagon was still on the ranch where she'd left it—Pru had her first misgiving when she realized Chance's truck was gone.

Even so, with Hope wedged against a hip, she banged at the door and, when no one answered, stalked right in. Her courage was up and she was not about to waste it. She was going to tell Chance the whole truth and ask him to forgive her.

Only…he wasn't there.

After checking both bunk rooms, she wanted nothing more than to sit herself down and have a good cry. Or to kick something in frustration!

She narrowed her gaze on a likely wastebasket. Then she spotted the rumpled flyer discarded on top and fetched it.

"Trinity Stampede. A rodeo!"

"Wodeo!" Hope repeated, grabbing for the flyer.

"R-r-rodeo," Pru automatically repeated, emphasizing the correct pronunciation as she realized the rough stock events would take place that very day.

She checked the closet. This wasn't Chance's room—no fancy shirts. Maybe he hadn't gone off to the stupid rodeo, after all. Maybe. But the terrible feeling was only growing stronger.

She ran to the other bunk room, Hope giggling at what she obviously thought was a game.

Chance's shirts and jeans were there. His chaps and spurs weren't.

"Double damnation, Chance Quarrels! If you go kill yourself riding a bronc in your condition, I'll never forgive you!"

"F'rgive!" Hope chirped.

"I know you don't get it yet, Squirt, but I'm talking about your daddy."

Pru gave her daughter a loving squeeze and left the bunkhouse, grateful to see a friendly face on the person heading toward them.

"Josie!" she called. "Where is everyone?"

"Bart and Moon-Eye and Daniel went to pick up the horses. I can't believe one of you rode Juniper. The blue roan."

"That would be Chance."

"Oh, thank God." Josie stopped before them and

tickled Hope's knee. "He's used to dealing with orneriness."

"So there's something wrong with that horse?"

"She's mostly green and can be spooky. A few weeks back a hired hand rode her without permission—"

"The Dagget kid?"

"That's the one."

In a town as small as Silver Springs, everyone knew when someone died, especially the way that kid had. Being dragged to death…Pru shivered and gave her own daughter an extra hug for good measure.

Cause enough for Hope to push at her. "Down, M'ma! Down!"

Pru gave way and followed the toddler toward the corral. "What about the others? Where are they?"

"Will said something about personal business that needed taking care of," Josie said. "He left before we heard from you yesterday. Then Kleef Hatsfield just up and disappeared without a word. Bart's none too happy about that, I can tell you. I think he's going to give Hatsfield his walking papers when he gets back."

Hope stood grasping the fencing, fascinated by a sorrel mare with a flaxen mane and tail inside the corral. Pru stood directly behind her.

"What about Chance?" she asked.

Josie shrugged. "This morning his truck was gone. It had us kind of worried, but then we figured he went for you."

"I wish." Pru shook her head. "I'm worried, Josie. Really worried. I keep getting the feeling that something's not right. I found a flyer for the Trinity rodeo, and Chance's chaps and spurs are gone.''

"Uh-oh. You don't think—"

"I'm afraid I do. I have this growing sense of doom that I can't shake—"

"But the kidnappers are behind bars."

"There's someone else. I guess I was too emotionally overcome to realize it yesterday. I don't believe it's either Silky or Ray," she said, shaking her head. "He calls himself the Cowboy Poet."

"Cowboy Poet?" Josie echoed. "I don't understand."

"The poet is determined to stop Chance from testifying. He seems to know Chance's every move and has been sending him these weird warnings about The Cowboy Code." Her chest tightened. "And every time Chance ignores it, something bad happens. I have to go after him."

"Not alone. Who knows what kind of trouble you might find at the other end of a four-hour drive?"

"I'm not waiting for Bart."

"How about me?" Josie offered. "I know my way around a rodeo. But you'd better leave Hope here. Felice will be thrilled to watch her. And Lainey. And, unless I miss my guess, even old Emmett."

"That would be best."

As much as Pru hated to be separated from Hope even for a minute after what she'd gone through, she wasn't about to put her child in danger again.

"Hey, Quarrels, it's been too long!"

Canvasing the rodeo grounds for a couple of familiar faces, Chance turned to see chute boss Joe

Hill, a small man who, despite his pop-bottle glasses, never missed a thing.

"What?" Chance asked. "A man can't take off a few weeks to relax?"

Joe's glasses reflected the waning sun as he stared at Chance's bruised face. "Yeah, you look like you been relaxin'." He raised his eyebrows.

Chance forced a grin. "But she was worth it."

Joe guffawed. "Well, now that's a whole different story."

As chute boss, Joe Hill oversaw the operation inside the rodeo arena. He coordinated which cowboys and their mounts would be released from which bucking chutes and when. A good man for some information.

"Say," Chance said real casual-like, "you haven't seen Will Spencer today, have you?"

"Billy-Boy? Yeah, he's around here someplace, maybe lookin' over the stock. He's goin' for All-Around today. Never thought I'd see him on no bull again."

"He made me think he was done with competing," Chance agreed. He himself had only entered saddle bronc so that he could move behind the scenes at will. "But you know, where women are concerned..."

"Women?"

"Silky...the big-haired blonde...only has those doe eyes for winners."

Joe sobered. "That Silky—she's a bad one. Will oughta stay as far away from her as he can get."

Not what Chance had been expecting to hear. "Why? What do you know about her?"

''That she's a damn tramp with no heart. Remember on the Fourth when Will got gored so bad?''

''Yeah, I remember.''

''That same night, when Will was laid up in critical condition in the hospital, I seen her bellying up to the bar with another cowboy.''

''Who?''

''Beats me,'' Joe said. ''Some guy with a big mustache is all I remember.''

Kleef? Chance wondered. Could it be? Or could it have been Ray. Though, since Ray worked for a stock supplier, Joe would probably know him.

Trying not to arouse any suspicions, Chance played it cool. ''I'd better get going and psyche myself into this thing.''

''A little meditation goes a long way to steady the nerves,'' Joe said agreeably. ''If I see Billy-Boy, I'll tell him you're lookin' for him.''

''No, don't. I'm hoping to surprise him.''

He was going over to the livestock and horse barns in hopes of finding Will right away. The sooner the better.

''You got it, Chance,'' Joe said, taking his departure. ''And good luck up there.''

''Thanks.''

Not that Chance expected to win or cared if he did. The only prize he coveted for the evening would be handing over the Cowboy Poet to the Sheriff's Department. Only then would he feel that everyone he cared about would be safe from the bastard's reach.

Chance had made up his mind. If he couldn't pin the Cowboy Poet as the third man in the robbery tonight, he would call the prosecutor to say he couldn't testify, after all. That he'd made up the story. That it had all been a big mistake.

He could hardly stand the thought of letting a death go, but worse would be for him to cause a second.

If he had only himself to worry about, that would be one thing. But there was Pa...Bart and his kids...Felice and Moon-Eye...Pru and Squirt...he couldn't put any of them in further danger for his sake.

At the first livestock barn he set his sights for Will, but couldn't spot him and so went on, all the while playing head games with himself, envisioning Pru holding Squirt...little Hope...his daughter.

He was still getting used to the idea.

And he was beginning to see how difficult it would have been for Pru to tell him. But life wasn't made up of easy choices. She'd said she'd tried, and he guessed she had.

*Chance Quarrels, you're a complicated man,* she'd told him. *But you're the only man I've ever loved. The only man I've ever wanted to be with. I waited for you—*

That time, he'd cut off what she'd been trying to say with a kiss.

And then later...

*But about the last time you were gone, Chance, there's something I have to tell you.*

As he jostled through the growing crowd, Pru's words rang in his head. As did his own.

*No, Miss Prudence, you don't. You don't have to tell me anything. Just love me now. That's all I ask.*

And hadn't she done just that?

If only her timing hadn't been off. Two years off.

A preacher's daughter pregnant out of wedlock. Even a wild child such as Pru had to have had trouble dealing with her situation, especially alone.

Thing was, she wouldn't have faced it alone if she'd come to him.

That she hadn't made him sick at heart.

Arriving at the big livestock barn, he forced Pru out of mind and concentrated on his mission.

And was well rewarded, for if his eyes didn't deceive him, there, at the other end, stood one of his quarries...just not the one he'd expected to find.

Even as he thought it, Kleef Hatsfield turned away and disappeared into the crowd.

"DOUBLE DAMNATION!" Enveloped in steam, Pru yelled as she got a good look under the hood of her station wagon. A hose had split and antifreeze was spitting all over the engine. "Bucket of bolts."

This time she did kick out in frustration, the tire being the recipient of her ill humor.

"You'd better watch it or we'll get a flat next," Josie warned her.

"I don't know how you can joke about it. Two-thirds of the way there and now look at us."

"Calm down." Josie pointed. "There's a gas station just down the road apiece."

Pru slammed the hood and checked her watch. "Let's get going, then. We'll be lucky if we slide into Trinity before the rodeo events start."

Luckily the weather was cool, the walking easy, the distance short. But when they got to the gas station, they found the mechanic had gone home early.

"Great!" Pru said, worry eating at her. "Now what? Anyplace we can rent a car around here?"

The guy, whose tag said his name was Waldo, looked at her as if she were nuts. Right. Rent a car in rural New Mexico.

"So we'll buy antifreeze," Josie said. "And we'll need water. And how about duct tape? Do you have any around."

"Yeah, but it belongs to the shop," Waldo said. "It's not for sale."

"You really want to leave two women stranded along the road?"

In the end Waldo closed up shop long enough to whip them back down the road to the station wagon. Josie wound the duct tape around and around the split in the hose, then added a mixture of antifreeze and water through the reserve.

Limp with relief, Pru waved off Waldo a few minutes later.

"Bye! Thanks! Now let's see how far the bucket of bolts gets us." She slid behind the wheel. "I can't believe how resourceful you are."

"When I was a kid, I had to help keep ranch equipment running. Mom and I ran a small spread practically alone until she died last year."

"Oh, Josie, I'm sorry."

"Thanks. It's getting easier."

How easy could it be losing someone you loved? Pru wondered. She'd lost Chance, but he was still alive, and she felt devastated. Judging by the way her feelings for him had remained so intense for so long, she couldn't imagine them dimming.

Trying to get her mind off it, she asked, "What happened to the ranch?"

"Nothing yet. But I'll have to figure out what to

do with the land eventually. For now, someone else is taking care of the place.''

''Cattle?''

''Horses.''

''Ah, I get it. That's why you're the Curly-Q's wrangler.'' Pru took a deep breath. ''You're also a good friend, Josie, one I can count on, just like Alcina.''

''The Three Musketeers.'' Josie laughed. ''To the rescue!''

Sobering at the reminder of their mission, Pru said, ''But there's only two of us.''

''Chance will be all right.''

Pru took heart in the reassurance until they hit a traffic slowdown. A multicar accident. She kept looking at her watch as if she could freeze time.

''What do you plan to do once we get to the Stampede?'' Josie asked. ''Other than stopping Chance from killing himself by riding when he shouldn't.''

''Look for the Cowboy Poet—he'll be there.''

''But you don't know what this guy looks like.''

''Maybe not. Then, again,'' Pru said thoughtfully, ''maybe I do. Maybe we both do.''

''Hmm. He could have been right under our noses all along,'' Josie admitted. ''If it happened to me…''

Barely a quarter of an hour before show time, they arrived at the Trinity Stampede grounds. The lot was bulging with vehicles, but Pru was determined to find herself a parking spot if she had to park on top of a truck. In the end they left the station wagon alongside the exit lane. Taking a chance on it being towed didn't seem too important right now.

They practically ran through the parking lot, then got caught up in the crowd. The carnival area was overflowing. And as they waited in line at the rodeo box office for tickets to the evening's events, the fanfare began.

A musical introduction was followed by the announcer saying, "Cowboys and cowgirls...welcome to the Thirteenth Annual Trinity Stampede."

"Uh-oh," Josie muttered. "Too late to stop Chance from riding."

Pru's heart fell. She'd never get back to the "cowboy shrine"—the area behind the chutes where all the competitors gathered to wait for their turn. A quick prayer was all she could do for Chance.

The announcer was saying, "Tonight...the rough stock events. Bareback...saddle bronc...and bull riding. We have a spectacular show in store for you, so give our contestants a big Southwestern welcome!"

The audience cheered and stomped and clapped and whistled as Pru and Josie found some seats, halfway back but near the center of the arena.

"Let's get right on with our first event!" the announcer enthused. "Bareback riding."

Heart heavy with worry over Chance, Pru barely listened as he droned on. She concentrated on searching the crowd for a familiar face. Next to her, Josie was doing the same.

"First out of the chutes," the announcer said, "Billy-Boy Spencer riding Torch Job!"

Hearing Will's name startled Pru. "What?"

She grabbed onto Josie's arm. The woman had stiffened but for a different reason. As the chutes opened and Will came flying out on an Appaloosa, Pru glanced away from the arena to her friend, whose gaze was fixed on someone in the crowd.

"See the man over there—dressed in black, handlebar mustache?"

Pru followed suit, scanning faces until she found him. "Isn't he a hired hand on the Curly-Q?"

"Sure is. Chance hired him, too." Even as the buzzer sounded, ending Will's eight-second ride, Josie identified him. "That's Kleef Hatsfield."

## Chapter Fourteen

He'd lost Kleef Hatsfield in the crowd.

Ten minutes to go before saddle bronc riding began. Chance warily checked the audience now and then, but never spotted the hired hand again.

Several cowboys milled around the readying area behind the bucking chutes, pacing off their nerves and checking over their equipment. More sat their saddles and stretched, then kicked out with their feet in their stirrups, imitating the spurring action they'd need to impress the judges. Others danced around or did abbreviated jumping jacks to keep their muscles from tightening in the cold.

Earlier, just before he'd been scheduled to ride in the bareback competition, Will had shown too late for Chance to corner him. Will had seen him, though, and, his smile tight, had waved before mounting Torch Job. He'd scored an eighty-four—high enough to win the event—before disappearing, as well.

To avoid him, Chance wondered, or to find Kleef?

He spotted his old acquaintance the moment Will returned to the cowboy shrine for the second event. The horses were already being moved from the holding pens and down the lane toward the bucking chutes. Will, too, was looking out over the crowd, as if he were searching for someone.

It was now or never.

"Hey, Will, good ride in the bareback. Congratulations."

"Chance!" Will wiped his mouth with the back of his glove. "Lucky is all. I'm surprised to see you, after everything that happened in the last couple of days."

"I've been hurt worse. You, too. I thought you were giving it up."

"I guess it's in the blood."

"Rodeo?" Chance asked, pausing for pure effect. "Or Silky?"

"What?"

"You haven't forgotten about Silky, have you, Will?" Chance figured he would be direct to a certain point, put some doubt in Will's mind without making any accusations. "She wouldn't like that, even if she did leave you after you were gored so bad that you wanted to quit the sport."

"I had a change of heart. So did she." Will glanced back at the crowd and seemed mesmerized for a moment by what he saw.

"Give it up," Chance suggested. "Silky's in jail. And my daughter's home safe."

Will whipped his head around to face Chance. Eyes wide, he said, "I...I don't know what you're talking about."

"That's good, Will. Real good. If it's true."

Deliberately turning his back on the man, Chance moved away and started his warm-up exercises. He could practically feel the nerves oozing out of the cowboy, like a live wire stretched between them. He grimaced at the comparison. He'd taken those pills Doc Baxter had forced on him, but still his shoulder sang to him every now and then.

The saddle bronc competition commenced. Will had drawn the seventh ride. A horse named Desperado. Chance might smile at the irony if so much weren't riding on his making Will play his hand if he was the Cowboy Poet.

Nerves were eating Will up. Chance could see it. The horse could feel it. The moment Will set down on his back, Desperado practically climbed the chute walls. Then the flank man told him to wait while he adjusted the horse's halter. Finally Will gave the nod and the gate opened, but too slowly for Desperado, who turned off-kilter and nearly unseated Will. The cowboy couldn't catch the rhythm, couldn't spur clean. An unexceptional ride with a score of sixty-three.

Chance watched Will as long as he could before the cowboy disappeared, but he was number nine in the lineup and needed to heed what he was doing.

Holding on to the slats, he took one last look around the audience before climbing into the chute. At first he thought he was seeing things. That his imagination was playing tricks on him. Then he realized Pru was really there, Josie next to her, both women waiting to watch him ride.

And over to their far right, Kleef Hatsfield stood, eyeing the two women.

Chance's mouth went dry. What the hell was Pru thinking of, coming after him? He was playing a dangerous game and didn't need to be worrying about her.

"Hey, Chance, mount up."

Climbing into the chute, he slipped his legs around Dangerous Illusion. He smashed his hat down hard over his forehead, took a deep breath, then nodded.

The gate swung open and his horse reared, feet pawing the air before slamming to the ground, throwing Chance slightly off balance. But he regained his seat even as his mount shot into the arena.

Left hand in the air despite the pain it caused him, Chance concentrated on that spurring action. He nearly clicked his spurs together behind him as the horse reached the top of his arc, then swept his feet forward as the horse's hooves touched the ground. Over and over he spurred…eight long seconds until the buzzer sounded.

Chance took a flying leap from his mount and landed on one hip. He used the momentum to roll to his knees and up to his feet. Right shoulder out of joint and heart palpitating again, he scrambled for the arena fence, then hung on by his left hand only, in an effort to keep himself upright. His head went light, and he lost his knees for a second. He remained on his feet by sheer will and by the grace of the fence that he clung to.

Within seconds the roar of the crowd turned his focus to the scoreboard. It flashed ninety-one. Not bad for an injured man, he thought with a grin. Best score so far—maybe even a winner.

One moment of glory…then his world righted and he remembered why he was there. He left the arena, cradling his right arm and pulled shoulder, his first thought to get to Pru and Josie, warn them off and send them packing.

But when he glanced back to find them in the crowd, both their seats were empty.

"IF YOU FIND HATSFIELD, keep him in sight but don't let him see you," Pru told Josie as they left the building. "Whatever you do, don't get too close."

"Yes, Mom."

"Jo-o-osie…"

"Don't worry about me," Josie insisted. "I know how to take care of myself. I'll meet you back at the box office in twenty minutes. No later, or I'll start worrying."

"We'll be there."

Pru was set on finding Chance, on sharing her theory about the Cowboy Poet and on informing him that Kleef Hatsfield was here.

She was also set on telling him the whole truth and only prayed he would listen.

The competitors used a door around the back side of the arena. She headed in that direction, meaning to be waiting for Chance when he exited. But a crowd of mostly young women blocked her path. The buckle bunnies were waiting to catch themselves cowboys for the night.

Intent on finding her own cowboy, Pru saw her opening.

All she had to do was circle the horse barn and she could at least get right up to the fence on the other side. Suddenly she wished her partner hadn't volunteered to play spy. Being a top barrel racer, Josie probably knew the gatekeepers and could get the two of them inside. Or at least on the other side of that fence.

As she rounded the barn, she spotted a couple of cowboys cutting through the area. The night was dark, the lighting inadequate.

Uneasy, she called, "Chance?"

"I'll give you a chance, darlin'," one cowboy said.

Not liking his suggestive tone of voice, she briskly said, "I'm looking for Chance Quarrels."

"I'm sorry it ain't me," replied the other.

"Yeah, me, too," she muttered, as yet another man stepped out of the shadows and into her path. She said, "Excuse me," and tried to move around him.

He turned with her.

Pulse zinging a warning, she whipped her head up to give him what for, only to have her throat close up tight.

She was staring into a bandanna-covered face....

TRYING TO MANIPULATE his shoulder back in place as he left the building, Chance was perturbed when one of the young workers got in his way.

"Mr. Quarrels, I hope to rodeo as good as you someday. You got any advice for me?"

"Sure. Work hard and live clean."

Anxious to get to Pru and Josie, Chance tried to circle the kid, who latched on to his arm.

"Wait a minute. I got something for you." The kid held out a familiar-looking envelope. "Some guy gave me this for you."

"Who?"

The kid shrugged. With trepidation, Chance opened the missive.

### The Cowboy Code Ignored
### by the Cowboy Poet

When the Cowboy Code gets ignored,
Someone is bound to get gored.
If you'd rather it was you instead of Pru,
Come direct to livestock barn number two.

''Is something wrong, Mr. Quarrels?'' the kid called after him as Chance raced through the back gate.

He passed cowboys milling around, many of them flirting with the rodeo groupies. Desperate, he kept working his shoulder until he felt it slide back into place. Now if only it would stay there, he prayed, as he passed the horse barn.

The crowd thinned out to a few stragglers. Chance figured any action in the livestock area would be in barn one. Normally both barns were only filled for the timed events, which had taken place the evening before. So barn two should be empty. Private.

*Dangerous.*

Did the Cowboy Poet really intend to kill Pru? Chance wondered. Or just him?

His heart thundered with fear for her.

He knew it had come to murder at last. He'd been warned over and over and hadn't backed out of testifying. Now it might be too late.

Pru couldn't die. He couldn't let her be victimized any further because of him. She had to be all right—they might not have a future together, but he still loved her. And she had their little girl to raise.

The image of Pru and Squirt together drove him faster.

Why couldn't Pru have told him? Why had she distrusted him, assumed he wouldn't do right by her and her child? Chance didn't know if he'd ever get over that particular heartbreak.

If he was lucky enough to be alive when the dust settled, that was.

Livestock barn two stood like a threatening entity

against the dark sky, dim light inside making the windows glow like waiting eyes....

Where would the poet be waiting for him? Chance wondered. And how could he get the drop on the bastard?

Thinking fast, he looked up. The doors to the hayloft stood open. And the hay truck was parked practically underneath them.

Stealthily moving to the truck, he looked over the bed where several bales stood. He glanced into the cab and spotted a coiled rope on the passenger side floor. Throwing it over his shoulder, he then searched behind the seats for some kind of tool that he could use as a weapon.

The very thing practically jumped out at him, and Chance began to believe in the poetic justice that the villain had been preaching at him....

He took the tool and wedged its length through his belt and against his back, then hauled himself up onto the truck bed. Looping the rope, he judged the distance to the hayloft and only hoped he could get there without alerting the man inside. He clambered onto one of the bales to get closer—the opening was now only a half dozen feet above.

Then he whirled the rope and lassoed a grappling hook jutting directly above the opening. He tightened the loop and, praying that he had the strength left, hauled himself up. Ignoring his protesting shoulders—both of them—he set himself down on the loft floor.

Pain flared from the infection, then dissipated quickly. He tested his right shoulder. Though a little weak, it was functional.

A noise ahead alerted him to another presence.

"Settle down," came the muffled male command, "or I'll finish you off now."

Chance silently slipped between bales until he could see them—the Cowboy Poet, his back turned, Pru in his grasp, a gun in his free hand. They stood mere feet from the edge of the hayloft. Snorting and pawing sounds from below told Chance that this barn wasn't empty of livestock, after all. At least one bull roamed the pens.

The plan suddenly coming clear in his mind, Chance felt his gut tighten.

"Chance won't do it," Pru was saying. "You won't get away with this."

"He won't have a choice. If he wants you to live, he'll sacrifice himself."

"You crazy bastard! Give it up! He's not going to jump down there."

But the poet didn't seem to be listening to her. "I know firsthand what a bull can do to a man," he said, "so you'd better hope it outright kills him. Your lover will be here soon, so we'll just see who is right about what he will or won't do for love."

Finally, thought Chance, he knew the man's identity.

From the shelter of a bale, he called out, "I'm here now…Will. Or should I call you the Cowboy Poet?"

Will Billy-Boy Spencer flipped around. Pru tried to break free, but he held her fast. Using his gun hand, he pulled down the bandanna, at last revealing his face. Then he aimed the barrel of the six-shooter at her.

His expression grim, he said, "You still surprise me, Chance."

"And you're still predictable, Will, using women and children to get what you want. And I suppose you'll just let Pru go, if I do jump down there and let myself be gored to death, right?" When Will didn't answer, Chance said, "That's what I thought."

"I tried not to hurt you or anyone else, Chance, really. But you just wouldn't cooperate. All I wanted was for you to back out of testifying. Why couldn't you just cooperate?"

"Because I have a conscience. Obviously something you know nothing about. If I backed out, the death of that security guard would have haunted me forever."

"No one was supposed to get hurt at the bank."

"Tell that to his widow!"

A flash of guilt actually crossed Will's features, and his gun hand trembled and dropped. Chance assessed the possibility of talking his way out of this, but didn't think the odds were with him. Certain that Will didn't want to kill him or Pru, he was equally certain the man had grown desperate.

"It all started with you, Chance," Will said. "You gave me the idea for the robbery. I went to Tunney and Moreno after overhearing the three of you laughing and joking about it." He was waving the gun around freely now. "I figured I wasn't going to rodeo again, and those two were desperate enough to team up with me if I figured it all out. How else was I going to make a living?"

"Hard work. But I knew you weren't a day job man, Will," Chance said. "So why don't you be honest? You're willing to take money that doesn't belong to you—and kill if necessary—and all for a woman who isn't worth it. Silky.''

"She is *mine* again."

"Was, until she put herself behind bars. And she was with you only because of the money."

"That's a damn lie! She always loved me, but she grew up dirt poor," Will said defensively. "She couldn't stand any more of that."

"So you got involved in a bank robbery…in a man's death…for love?" Pru asked, sounding shocked. "You don't know what love is!"

"But Chance here does, don't you?" Will asked. "You'd do anything for Pru, even die for her."

At which point Pru burst into loud sobs. "He doesn't love me! He used me!"

Appalled, Chance said, "Pru, I—"

"Don't. Just don't." Pru gave him the evil eye. "Maybe it's better this way," she said, her voice trembling as she made a goofy face at him that Will couldn't see. Her tone exaggerated, she said, "Why don't you just jump—" she nodded her head toward Will "—and get it over with!"

Realizing she wanted him to play along—that she meant jump Will, not jump down into the pens—Chance said, "Maybe I should let Will throw you to the bull." He was inching closer as he spoke.

Obviously taken aback by the unexpected argument, Will pointed his gun at Chance and said, "Hey, wait a minute!"

"Coward!" Pru yelled, and Chance could see she was working up to make her move.

"Witch!"

"Just stop—"

Pru elbowed Will hard, and Chance made a dive for his gun, grabbing the man's wrist with both hands. The blast shook the rafters and the bull below. The animal let out a bellow nearly as loud as Will's. Will let go of Pru so that he could better fight to regain control of the weapon in his hand.

Chance whirled Will around, aware they were getting closer to the loft's edge. Thinking fast, he kept hold of the gun and Will's hand with one hand and reached behind him. Grabbing the makeshift weapon he'd found in the truck, he flipped on the cattle prod and jabbed the points in Will's hip.

A jolt shook them both—from Will to the gun metal to Chance, whose heart kick started alarmingly. But Will's hand opened and the gun fell to the pens below.

Will lunged at Chance, knocking away the cattle prod. It rolled across the floor toward Pru while they rolled over a hay bale, Will landing on top.

Fist closed he struck out. Chance jerked his head out of the way, and Will's fist sank into the bale next to his ear. Suddenly Will spasmed and popped upright.

Pru was behind him, hanging on to the cattle prod like a sword. "Give it up, Will!"

While the cowboy was distracted, Chance took his best shot, his fist connecting with Will's jaw. The man's head snapped and he took a step back. Eyes opening in surprise, Will tried to catch himself as he lost his balance and, limbs flailing, did a Texas two-step right over the edge of the loft. He scrambled for a handhold and found it, then dangled by one hand.

The bull below was making a ruckus, snorting and tearing around his pen.

"Help me!" Will begged.

Kneeling, Chance reached out. "Not that you deserve it."

Will clasped the offered hand, but Chance felt his shoulder separating once more.

"Can't...hold you," he grunted.

Will clambered halfway onto the loft...and tried sending Chance over the side in his stead. Shoulder separated, Chance knew he would never be able to save himself if he lost his foothold.

Will spasmed again and let go when Pru got him with the cattle prod. He grabbed for her ankle, the rocky motion sealing his fate even as she jumped out of his reach. With a shout that echoed through the rafters, he hurtled downward, crashing into the pen. The bull's bellow zinged up Chance's spine.

From the ruckus below, he knew Will was a goner.

Seeing that Pru was about to investigate, Chance wrapped his still-functional left arm around her and pulled her close and thanked the Almighty that they had both come out of this alive.

PRU WAITED AT THE HOSPITAL until dawn, until she knew Chance would be all right. Josie had already left with Bart hours before. And Kleef Hatsfield, an investigator who'd been hired to keep an eye on the prosecution's star witness lest he do a disappearing act, had gone straight back to the Curly-Q to pack his things.

Exhausted, Pru finally headed for the ranch to pick up Hope. Felice insisted she stay for breakfast.

"What are we going to do with you two?" the housekeeper asked as Pru cleaned her plate, then

turned her attention to Hope's sticky hands and face.
"You worry us so."

"It's over," Pru assured her. "Finally. Now we
can all sleep at night."

Though how she would sleep not knowing what
the future held for them, Pru didn't know.

She thought nothing of the roar of a truck pulling
up, until Emmett walked in, saying, "The boy took
himself out of the hospital again!"

"Double damnation!"

"I can watch Hope a while longer," Felice suggested.

"No, but thank you."

Pru left the house, her daughter's hand in hers,
vaguely aware of being followed. She had only one
focus for the moment, and even with his face turning
terrible colors, the sight of him made her heart dance.

"Hey, Squirt. Pru."

"What are you doing here, Chance?" Pru demanded. "You were supposed to stay for observation
until tomorrow morning."

That was when Bart had planned on picking him
up to take him to the trial—a personal bodyguard
service.

"The only one I want to have observe me is you,"
Chance insisted. He removed his Stetson and crushed
it between both hands. The morning sun glinted gold
through his hair, which he'd neatly tied back from
his face. "I have to get this out before I lose my
nerve. Marry me, Pru."

The breath caught in her throat at the unexpected
proposal, and all she could manage to croak out was,
"Why?"

"What?" Chance grinned. "Squirt there is a mighty good reason."

Her heart fell. "That's what I figured." She started to move past him, practically dragging Hope toward the station wagon.

"M'ma, no!"

Hope dug in her heels long enough for Chance to get between them and the vehicle.

"Hey," he protested, "what's going on here? I thought you'd want me to make an honest woman of you."

Pru stopped and faced him. "Actually, that's exactly what I was afraid of."

He scowled. "So you don't want to be married—at least not to me. I guess you really *don't* trust me."

"I *do* trust you, Chance. That's the problem."

He stared at her a minute as if she were crazy. And maybe she was. Pru picked up Hope, as if their daughter could protect her from her own tumultuous feelings.

Chance glanced from her to the little girl and shook his head. "I'm missing something here."

"I trust you always to do the right thing, Chance," Pru said. "I guess deep inside I always have. I knew if I told you that I was pregnant, you would marry me to give our child your name—"

"Whoa!"

"Let me finish." She had to get it out now, all of it. She took a big breath and ignored the cotton-candy feel to her mouth. "You want the whole truth about why I didn't tell you about Hope? I made all kinds of excuses, and while there was some validity to them, the real reason was that I was afraid, Chance. I was afraid that you would want to marry me out of obligation because I was pregnant. I didn't want to trap you. I wanted you to want *me*.''

"I *do* want you!" Chance practically yelled, at which point Hope screwed up her face as if she was about to cry. "Hey, Squirt, I didn't mean to scare you," he said, touching her face gently until she relaxed. "Or your mom." He met Pru's gaze with one as sincere as she'd ever seen on him. "Wanting you was all I could think about when I was gone. I was stupid to fight it—I admit that. But I didn't want to come home empty-handed, either. I wanted to prove that I was worth something. I love you, Pru, not as Hope's mother, but as the only woman I could imagine sharing my life with!''

"Your life?" Her heart soared. "No more going off where the wind blows?''

Chance shook his head. "Not unless you come with me, Prunella. I've changed, and I'll spend the rest of my life proving it to you…if you'll let me.''

"Forever after?''

"Forever after.''

With that he kissed her, careful not to crush their wiggling daughter between them.

While Pru was carried away by Chance's kiss, as always, she couldn't help but hear old Emmett tell Felice, "Looks like the boy really has changed.''

"I knew my Chance had it in him all along," Felice said with pride in her voice.

And deep in her heart Pru admitted that she had, as well.

## *Epilogue*

"I now pronounce you husband and wife...."

Even before the Reverend Brewster Prescott could say, "You may now kiss the bride," to his new son-in-law, Chance did.

Pru lost herself in her husband's arms, coming to only when she realized the thundering in her ears wasn't just her wildly beating heart but the applause of the whole town. Giddy and a little embarrassed, she stepped away from Chance. Heat stole up her neck.

"Why, Miss Prudence," Chance murmured, flashing her a bedroom smile that zapped her all the way to her toes.

Then he offered her his arm, and they led the way down the aisle—Bart, as best man, and Alcina, as maid of honor, right behind them. Passing her happily weeping mother Naomi and Justine and her family, Pru grinned like a fool.

Outside the church they were surrounded by family and friends, old neighbors and new acquaintances. Everyone had turned out for the wedding that they'd put together in a few short weeks.

Everyone already in town or in the vicinity, that was.

One very important person was missing, and Pru tensed as Chance looked around again and muttered to himself, "I guess I never was important to Reed, after all."

She and Alcina exchanged glances, and Pru noted the disappointment her best friend was trying to hide. Pru had fun teasing Alcina about her ancient, school-girl crush on Reed every once in a while, but she hadn't known her feelings might still be very real.

"I don't understand it," Emmett complained, holding on to one of Hope's hands, while Felice held the other, the little girl having taken to them both. "Reed assured me he'd be here. This isn't like him."

"Maybe he changed his mind about coming back to Silver Springs, period," Alcina said, an underlying tension to her light tone.

"I don't believe it." Emmett shook his head. "Not Reed. Solid as a rock, that boy. He'll be here. Something important must have come up is all...."

TWENTY-THREE MILES north of Silver Springs, Reed Quarrels was hunkered down, facing the back of the Enchanted Highway Truck Stop building. He listened intently, blocked out the drone of the interstate, swore he heard another whine. This one sounded promising.

"C'mon, girl, come get it," he urged, his voice soft and even. Purposely unthreatening. "You know you want to."

A scratched-up nose pointed its way out from between two dumpsters, followed by a set of the most suspicious eyes he'd ever seen on a dog.

Reed crooned about the quality of the hamburger he'd torn into pieces and left barely a yard in front of him...the cool, sweet taste of the cup of water. He kept on issuing a stream of words, getting her used to the sound of his voice.

The dog would have to approach him to eat and drink. And she was getting desperate. Her ribs were showing, part of her ear had been bitten off and was infected, and she was limping. He'd spotted her rooting around the dumpsters for food when he'd stopped for gas and a quick cup of coffee. That had been nearly two hours ago. He'd told the guy behind the counter about the dog, but the kid had merely shrugged his shoulders and muttered about it being a shame and all.

But Reed simply couldn't shrug his shoulders and drive away, even knowing that he was missing his younger brother's wedding.

His patience was finally rewarded when the dog approached him, her belly to the ground.

"You don't have to be afraid," he assured her, guessing she'd been the recipient of purposeful ill-treatment by some human. "Not of me. Never of me."

She gobbled down the burger and drank the water.

Reed pulled a reserve from his pocket. He held out a piece and waited. Making up her mind, the dog darted forward and grabbed it from his hand, then retreated a few steps to eat it, never taking her eyes from him.

Reed set down the last piece and carefully moved away and toward his pickup.

The dog hesitated only a second before finishing it off.

By then Reed was in the truck, behind the wheel. He'd left the passenger door open. Whistling softly, he patted the seat and said, "C'mon, girl, get in."

The dog hesitated only a second before leaping in and cowering on the floor.

Relieved that he wouldn't miss the wedding party, as well, Reed closed the door and started off for the ranch he had once sworn he would never work again.

\* \* \* \* \*

*Don't miss the exciting conclusion to*
SONS OF SILVER SPRINGS,

*THE RANCHER'S VOW,*

coming next month from
Harlequin Intrigue.

# Looking For More Romance?

Visit Romance.net

Look us up on-line at: http://www.romance.net

**Check in daily for these and other exciting features:**

**Hot off the press**

View all current titles, and purchase them on-line.

What do the stars have in store for you?

**Horoscope**

**Hot deals**

Exclusive offers available only at Romance.net

Plus, don't miss our interactive quizzes, contests and bonus gifts.

PWEB

# HEART OF THE WEST

# Every Man Has His Price!

Lost Springs Ranch was famous for turning young mavericks into good men. So word that the ranch was in financial trouble sent a herd of loyal bachelors stampeding back to Wyoming to put themselves on the auction block!